"I'm not going to attack you," Ren growled.

"M-more than you already have?"

"You're alive, aren't you?" he snapped. "At least for now."

Wrong choice of words, he realized. He was grimly aware that she was trembling now. He hated her terror and wanted to explain everything, but he didn't dare take the time.

"Look, I'm trying to help you. There are some nasty creatures out here after dark, not a few of them human. Trust me, sweetheart. I'm your best chance of getting out of this whole thing in one piece." In desperation he handed her an oversized T-shirt and shorts. Anything to cover her skimpy bikini.

When she didn't move, he grabbed the shorts and yanked them over her hips. She flinched when he touched the bare skin at her waist.

"If I had evil designs on you, don't you think I'd be taking your clothes *off,* not putting them on?" he drawled.

Dear Reader,

Readers often ask me where I find ideas for my books. I'm afraid I have no secret stash of ideas. For *High-Stakes Honeymoon,* I created a sibling for a favorite character of mine, Daniel Galvez, while I was writing a previous book. I didn't know anything about this sibling other than his name—Lorenzo "Ren" Galvez—and that he was very sexy, of course, and a scientist somewhere in Latin America.

And then I happened to catch a few minutes of a documentary about sea turtles in Costa Rica and I knew this was where I had to plunk Ren. I had to create a heroine just right for him, and I came up with Olivia Lambert, someone funny and smart but wracked with self-doubt. Olivia brings out all of Ren's protective instincts and she also proves herself to be brave and self-reliant.

I spent months immersing myself in the culture and the overwhelming beauty of Costa Rica. While I haven't actually visited yet, it's definitely on my life-list of travel destinations and I plan to go soon.

I hope you enjoy the journey!

RaeAnne Thayne

RaeAnne Thayne

HIGH-STAKES HONEYMOON

Silhouette®

Romantic

SUSPENSE

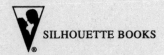

SILHOUETTE BOOKS

ISBN-13: 978-0-373-27545-8
ISBN-10: 0-373-27545-5

HIGH-STAKES HONEYMOON

Books by RaeAnne Thayne

Silhouette Romantic Suspense

The Wrangler and the Runaway Mom #960
Saving Grace #995
Renegade Father #1062
*The Valentine Two-Step #1133
*Taming Jesse James #1139
*Cassidy Harte and the Comeback Kid #1144
The Quiet Storm #1218
Freefall #1239
Nowhere To Hide #1264
†Nothing To Lose #1321
†Never Too Late #1364
The Interpreter #1380
High-Risk Affair #1448
Shelter from the Storm #1467
High-Stakes Honeymoon #1475

Silhouette Special Edition

Light the Stars #1748
Dancing in the Moonlight #1755
Dalton's Undoing #1764

*Outlaw Hartes
†The Searchers

RAEANNE THAYNE

finds inspiration in the beautiful northern Utah mountains, where she lives with her husband and three children. Her books have won numerous honors, including a RITA® Award nomination from Romance Writers of America and a Career Achievement Award from *Romantic Times BOOKreviews*. RaeAnne loves to hear from readers and can be reached through her Web site at www.raeannethayne.com or at P.O. Box 6682, North Logan, UT 84341.

Chapter 1

Paradise sucked.

Big-time.

Olivia Lambert sat on her damp towel, her hands clasped around her knees, watching the sun sink into the Pacific in a blaze of color. Palm fronds whispered a soft song overhead, the warm, impossibly blue ocean gently kissed the sand at her feet and a soft breeze danced across her skin.

Behind her, the thick, lush rain forest teemed with color and noise and life—bright birds, exotic butterflies, even a monkey or two.

As a honeymoon destination, this remote, wild corner of Costa Rica seemed perfect, especially staying in a guest villa on the estate of a reclusive billionaire. It was romantic, secluded, luxurious.

The only trouble was, she'd left her groom behind in Texas.

Olivia sighed, gazing out at the ripple of waves as she tried to drum up a little enthusiasm for the holiday that stretched ahead of her like the vast, undulating surface of the Pacific. She'd been here less than twenty-four hours and had nine more days to go, and at this point she was just about ready to pack up her suitcases and catch the next puddle jumper she could find back to the States.

She was bored and lonely and just plain miserable.

Maybe she should have invited one of her girlfriends to come along for company. Or better yet, she should have just eaten the cost of the plane tickets and stayed back in Fort Worth.

But then she would have had to face the questions and the sympathetic—and not so sympathetic—looks and the resigned disappointment she was entirely too accustomed to seeing in her father's eyes.

No, this way was better. If nothing else, ten days in another country would give her a little time and distance to handle the bitter betrayal of knowing that even in this, Wallace Lambert wouldn't stand behind her. Her father sided with his golden boy, his groomed successor, and couldn't seem to understand why she might possibly object to her fiancé cheating on her with another woman two weeks before their wedding.

It was apparently entirely unreasonable of her to expect a few basic courtesies—minor little things like fidelity and trust—from the man who claimed to adore her and worship the ground she walked on.

Who knew?

The sun slipped further into the water and she

sighed again, angry at herself. So much for her promise that she wouldn't brood about Bradley or her father.

This was her honeymoon and she planned to enjoy herself, damn them both. She could survive nine more days in paradise, in the company of macaws and howler monkeys, iguanas and even a sloth—not to mention her host, whom she had yet to encounter.

James Rafferty, whom she was meeting later for dinner, had built his fortune through online gambling and he had created an exclusive paradise here completely off the grid—no power except through generators, water from wells on the property. Even her cell phone didn't work here.

Nine days without distractions ought to be long enough for her to figure out what she was going to do with the rest of her life. She was twenty-six years old and it was high time she shoved everybody else out of the driver's seat so she could start picking her own direction.

Some kind of animal screamed suddenly, a high, disconcerting sound, and Olivia jumped, suddenly uneasy to realize she was alone down here on the beach.

There were jaguars in this part of the Osa Peninsula, she had read in the guidebook. Jaguars and pumas and who knew what else. A big cat could suddenly spring out of the jungle and drag her into the trees, and no one in the world would ever know what happened to her.

That would certainly be a fitting end to what had to be the world's worst honeymoon.

She shivered and quickly gathered up her things, shaking the sand out of her towel and tossing her sunglasses and paperback into her beach bag along with her cell phone that she couldn't quite sever herself from, despite its uselessness here.

No worries, she told herself. She seemed to remember jaguars hunted at night and it was still a half hour to full dark. Anyway, she had a hard time believing James Rafferty would allow wild predators such as that to roam free on his vast estate.

Still, she wasn't at all sure she could find her way back to her bungalow in the dark, and she needed to shower off the sand and sunscreen and change for dinner.

She had waited too long to return, she quickly discovered. She would have thought the dying rays of the sun would provide enough light for her to make her way back to her bungalow, fifty yards or so from the beach up a moderate incline. But the trail moved through heavy growth, feathery ferns and flowering shrubs and thick trees with vines roped throughout.

What had seemed lovely and exotic on her way down to the beach suddenly seemed darker, almost menacing, in the dusk.

Something rustled in the thick undergrowth to her left. She swallowed a gasp and picked up her pace, those jaguars prowling through her head again.

Next time she would watch the sunset from the comfort of her own little front porch, she decided nervously. Of course, from what the taciturn housekeeper who had brought her food earlier said, this dry sunset was an anomaly this time of year, given the daily rains.

Wasn't it just like Bradley to book their honeymoon destination without any thought that they were arriving in the worst month of the rainy season. She would probably be stuck in her bungalow the entire nine days.

Still grumbling under her breath, she made it only a few more feet before a dark shape suddenly lurched out of the gathering darkness. She uttered a small shriek of surprise and barely managed to keep her footing.

In the fading light, she could only make out a stranger looming over her, dark and menacing. Something long and lethal gleamed silver in the fading light, and a strangled scream escaped her.

He held a machete, a wickedly sharp one, and she gazed at it, riveted like a bug watching a frog's tongue flicking toward it. She couldn't seem to look away as it gleamed in the last fading rays of the sun.

She was going to die alone on her honeymoon in a foreign country in a bikini that showed just how lousy she was at keeping up with her Pilates.

Her only consolation was that the stranger seemed just as surprised to see her. She supposed someone with rape on his mind probably wouldn't waste time staring at her as if she were some kind of freakish sea creature.

Come on. The bikini wasn't *that* bad.

She opened her mouth to say something—she wasn't quite sure what—but before she could come up with anything, he gave a quick look around, then grabbed her from behind, shoving the hand not holding the machete against her mouth.

Panic spurted through her as he dragged her into the thick, lush rain forest. Her flip-flops almost fell off but she dug her toes into them as she stumbled after him until they were swallowed up by the jungle, the trail completely out of sight behind them.

After a moment, he stopped, holding her tightly against his hard chest as he stood motionless. She was aware of every single breath against her bare skin and could feel her own hitching in and out of her lungs.

She was going to hyperventilate. She could feel her hands start to go numb and her breathing accelerate. A whimper escaped her, and his grip tightened on her mouth. She could taste his skin, salty and masculine and foreign.

"Quiete," he ordered harshly in her ear and even Olivia, who had only pulled a C-minus in prep school Spanish, understood what he meant. She forced herself to breathe more slowly, evenly, though she could hear her pulse, loud and strident in her ear.

For what felt like forever, they stood locked together, unmoving. She was too afraid to struggle against the strong arms that held her, acutely aware of the machete he held at his side and of exactly how much damage that blade could do.

He spoke a few more low words to her in Spanish but she didn't understand what he wanted, any more than she could interpret the hoots and peeps and calls of the night creatures all around them.

He stiffened suddenly and in the distance she saw the beam of a flashlight coming from the trail. Whoever held it aimed it in their direction, but its light couldn't pierce the thick growth. She wanted to cry out, do anything to reveal their location, but she didn't dare, ever conscious of that machete.

A moment later, she heard loud voices saying something that sounded like curses in Spanish, before the light disappeared.

The man breathing raggedly behind her waited a few more seconds, then he growled something else she didn't understand in her ear, the normally fluid Spanish sounding guttural and sharp.

He dropped his hand, apparently expecting some kind of answer. She didn't have a clue what the question had been, which didn't seem to go over well with him. Her captor repeated the words, more harshly this time.

"I'm sorry," she whimpered. In the dim light, she saw the whites of his eyes as they widened.

"You're American?" he whispered. "I should have known."

He growled a long string of curses—pungent and raw and all too understandable.

"I'm sorry," she said again. "Please don't hurt me. Look, I have money in my bag and credit cards. Take them," she pressed, thrusting out her beach bag. "Please take them and let me go."

He grabbed the bag from her and rummaged through it, but apparently didn't find whatever he was seeking.

He lifted the machete and she swallowed a scream that ended in a gasp when he severed one of the long leather handles. He handed the mangled bag back to her and when she reached for it, he grabbed her wrists and tied the ruined handle around them.

Her heart plummeted to her feet when he took off again through the thick growth with his machete swinging, tugging her behind him with the improvised restraint.

"Please don't hurt me," she tried again. "My father will pay you anything you want."

She hoped, anyway.

Maybe Wallace would figure this was a fitting end to his total disappointment in his only child, that she die at the hands of a homicidal, machete-wielding maniac in the jungles of Costa Rica.

"It's too late for that. I'm in a boatload of trouble here and you just landed your little bikini-clad butt right in the middle of it."

As much as she wanted to, she couldn't contain her small sound of distress.

"Look, I won't hurt you." He paused and even through the darkness she could feel the heat of his look. "Unless you try to run, anyway. Believe it or not, I'm pretty certain you're far safer with me than you would be if I left you here."

She dug around in her psyche for any tiny kernel of courage and managed to find one in a dusty corner. "That's odd," she retorted through trembling lips, "considering I've been here an entire day and this is the first time a madman with a machete has dragged me into the jungle."

The momentary spurt of bravado disappeared when she heard a shriek nearby, then a swoop of wings and the unmistakably grim sound of something dying.

Her captor tugged her restraint and pushed on. "There are worse things on Suerte del Mar than a madman with a machete."

While her imagination tried to ponder what that might possibly be, he cut through the heavy growth, roughly parallel to the shore. He seemed to have eyes like the jaguar she had mistaken him for earlier. While she stumbled in her flip-flops over roots and small plants, he plowed through, the machete scything away as he tugged her inexorably toward some destination she could only guess at.

After a few more moments, he shifted direction and headed down toward the ocean.

"Where are you taking me?" she finally dared ask.

"Rafferty keeps his boat docked here. It's the only way we're getting away."

Oh, she didn't like the sound of that. "Please," she tried one more time. "Just leave me here. I'll only slow you down."

For about half a second, she thought he might be wavering, then he tugged her restraint. "Sorry, sweetheart. You don't have a choice anymore. Neither of us does."

He led her toward the dock she had noticed that afternoon when she had been soaking up the sun, feeling sorry for herself and thinking her life couldn't get much worse.

Ha!

Ren Galvez was totally screwed.

He figured it out the minute he walked into Suerte del Mar. He only intended to talk to Rafferty about tightening the leash on his dogs. Earlier in the day, he had seen the vicious one, the Doberman, within a few hundred yards of the nesting site just down the beach from Rafferty's estate.

He had warned the man and his goons repeatedly, and he was damn sick and tired of it.

He had planned to tell Jimbo that he was done playing nice. If Ren caught the dogs there again, he was going to start taking pictures and broadcasting them on every sea turtle blog and Web site he knew about.

That should have been enough to do the trick. Ren despised the man on several levels, but James Rafferty put up a good show of being the benevolent environmentalist, a billionaire dedicated to protecting the rain forest and the lush biodiversity of this largely undeveloped region of Costa Rica.

That image would be more than tarnished if Ren went public with pictures of Rafferty's guard dogs harassing nesting endangered sea turtles.

When he kayaked over from his research station down the coast, Ren only intended to talk to the man and warn him for the last time about the dogs.

He hadn't expected to walk into hell.

He blocked the grim images out and focused only on the job at hand, saving his own skin and that of the soft woman currently tethered to him, stumbling as she hurried to keep up.

"Can you slow down?" his captive said, her sultry, tequila voice breathless. "It's a little hard hiking in flip-flops."

He tightened his grip on the leather strap without risking a look in her direction. He couldn't afford to get distracted looking at the vast expanse of skin bared by her skimpy swimming suit.

She was stacked. The kind of lush, voluptuous figure that turned men's minds to mush and their bodies to putty.

Not his. Not now. He had other things to worry about than how long it had been since he'd had much interest in a woman's curves—and how inconvenient that he should take notice of *these* particular curves, when he ought to be more worried about saving both their skins.

"By now they've let the dogs loose after me. You might not care if Jimbo's Doberman takes a piece out of that pretty little rear of yours, but I can't say the same."

She stopped on the trail. "Dogs? Why would Rafferty

set dogs after you? What have you done, besides kidnap an innocent woman?"

"Nice try. You're not innocent or you wouldn't be hanging out with James Rafferty."

"I'm just a guest here. I haven't even met the man yet! I was invited to dinner at the house and was just returning to dress for it. He's going to be very upset if I don't show up."

"You don't know the half of it, sweetheart."

He thought of what he had heard her esteemed host say as he stood over the body of the woman he had just killed.

This was a nice appetizer for the entrée I have planned later, Rafferty had drawled in an ice-cold voice to the horror-stricken man on the lawn chair next to the dead woman. *Or perhaps I'll save the little blond cream puff for dessert.*

He'd been too busy trying to save his own hide to let the words sink in, until he realized the woman he bumped into on the trail must be Rafferty's next course.

He couldn't just leave her to face whatever Rafferty had planned for her. Blame it on this damn streak of chivalry he couldn't quite shake, but he wasn't about to leave her here to suffer the same fate as Rafferty's other hapless guest—or worse.

As soon as he reached the dock, he realized that apparently Suerte del Mar's famed luck didn't apply to him. He was screwed again—the man's elegant, outrageously expensive yacht, the *Buena Suerte,* was nowhere in evidence.

On the other hand, that might not be a bad thing. It meant Rafferty wouldn't be able to come after them, at least not by water. "Come on," he ordered his hostage.

"Where?"

"Rafferty keeps a kayak down here."

"You're just going to take it?"

He tried not to notice how soft and delectable she looked in that barely-there swimsuit. "I'll leave an IOU. You got any better ideas?"

"Yes. Leave me here!"

He didn't dignify that with an answer as they reached the sleek two-person sea kayak.

This kidnapping business was tricky stuff, he realized immediately. How was he supposed to haul the damn thing down to the surf while still holding his machete and the leather strap binding her hands?

He finally had to take a chance and toss the machete into the kayak and pull the craft one-handed down the sand while he dragged her along with the other hand.

It was hard, awkward work but adrenaline pushed him along, helped in large measure by the intense barking he could hear drawing closer.

"Get in," he growled, when they reached the waves.

She froze, and in the moonlight she lifted stricken, terrified eyes to him. He wanted to assure her everything would be all right but he didn't have time—and right about now, he needed somebody to convince *him* they would make it through this.

Instead, he picked her up and plopped her in the front cockpit, fastening the apron around her in one smooth motion.

"You're going to have to trust me, lady, as insane as that might seem right now. If you don't, we're both going to end up dead, I can promise you that."

"Please let me go," she begged again. "Please. I

won't tell anyone I saw you, I swear. I don't even know who you are or…or why you're running away."

She might not. But Rafferty certainly did. The gambling mogul would know as soon as his men found Ren's own kayak at the other end of the beach who had come to call—and who had witnessed the whole ugly business by the pool.

By now they had probably found it, complete with his research notebooks and his satellite phone in its watertight pouch, which would have come in mighty handy right about now.

Their only chance was to make it two miles down the coast to his research station and his Jeep so he could head to the little rural police outpost in the next village to report what he had seen.

If anybody would even believe him. After his wildness of the last few years, he didn't exactly have the greatest reputation among the villages on the Osa.

He pushed that depressing thought away as he towed the kayak out into the surf, then climbed in behind his hostage and started paddling like hell to get them away.

The woman was making small whimpers in front of him. He was sorry for her panic—terrifying a woman wasn't something that sat well with Neva Galvez's younger son.

His brother Daniel, the sturdy and honorable sheriff of Moose Springs, Utah, would probably frown on this whole business. But it couldn't be helped. Right now he didn't have breath left to explain anything. He could only work the oars with all his energy.

They made it to the point at the edge of the moon-shaped beach of the Suerte in half the time it would have normally taken him and only after they slid around it and out of sight of the estate did Ren begin to breathe a little easier.

They certainly weren't out of trouble yet. Rafferty's men had probably already found his kayak—easily identifiable to anyone around these parts—and figured out he was the idiot who had intruded on their boss's private little party. But the roads in this section of the Osa were wild and primitive, requiring four-wheel-drive most of the time. This was the rainy season, when the roads turned into big sloshy piles of mud.

He could kayak down the coast far more quickly than they could drive to his place.

He cursed himself all over again. None of this would have happened if he had just slipped back the way he had come as soon as he figured out what was going down at the hacienda's pool. Nobody would have even known he was there.

But seeing Rafferty standing over the body of a dead woman, the gun in his hand and the grisly hole in her forehead, had stunned him so much he had stood frozen like a damn piece of furniture as he watched Rafferty taunt the man tied to a lawn chair about the gambling debts he owed him and Rafferty's uniquely effective form of debt collection.

The shock wore off quickly, leaving hot dread in his gut as he realized what a mess he had stumbled into.

He had tried to back out quietly. He was used to stealth—hell, he could sneak up on a twelve-hundred-pound nesting leatherback without making a sound.

He would have probably made it, if a howler monkey hadn't chosen just that moment to come swinging through the trees and making a ruckus, giving away his position in the process.

One of the thugs Rafferty surrounded himself with had sighted him and he had given up on stealth and had just run like hell. A few moments later, he had stumbled onto the woman whose soft, hunched shoulders were currently trembling in front of him.

Ren sighed and slowed his frenetic paddling enough that he could catch his breath. They needed to hurry, but he could at least take a moment to allay her fears.

"Hold out your hands," he said.

She turned, flashing him a wide-eyed look of fright in the moonlight, and he felt like some kind of perverted rapist again.

"Come on. I told you I won't hurt you. If you promise not to jump out, I can untie you now."

After a moment's hesitation, she held out her trembling hands. Regretting her fear, he pulled his pocket knife out and cut through the leather binding her. She flexed her wrists and he thought maybe her big blue eyes lost a little of their panic.

"I'm Lorenzo Galvez. Ren. What's your name?"

"Olivia Lambert. My…my father will pay to have me home safely." Her voice faltered.

She had said that already, he remembered. And with that same note of doubt in her voice.

"You don't sound a hundred percent convinced of that, sweetheart."

"He will."

"He a gambler?"

She blinked, her lashes looking impossibly thick

and dark in the moonlight reflecting off the water. "Excuse me?"

"I'm just trying to figure out how you got messed up with Rafferty, Olivia Lambert. What are you doing at Suerte del Mar?"

"I'm…I'm here on my honeymoon."

A raw, strangled laugh escaped him and he was tempted to smack the paddle against his head a few times.

Could his life *get* any more delightful?

"Your honeymoon. Perfect. So not only will we have a homicidal gazillionaire after us but a frantic groom looking for his bride."

She made a sound he couldn't interpret, but it was cut off when a dark shape moved past them in the water, brushing his paddles as it went.

"What was that?" she gasped.

He peered into the inky water. "Nothing to worry about. My guess is a *triaenodon obesus*. White-tipped reef shark. Around here they call them *cazón coralero trompacorta*. That's what it looked like from here, but I could be wrong."

"A…a shark?"

Her voice wobbled. Afraid she was about to cry, he hurried to reassure her.

"They're relatively harmless. Pretty easygoing. Sometimes they even let divers hand-feed them. I'm a little surprised he would come this close to the surface, since they usually stay pretty close to the substrate at the ocean floor where they feed, but he was probably just curious about what we might be doing up here."

"Are…are you a diver?"

He had to admit, she was taking all of this remarkably well, though he could sense every time the moments of panic seemed to creep in. As a scientist, he had to admire any creature that could adapt to its circumstances.

"When I have to be," he answered. "I'm a research biologist. I study the nesting habits of sea turtles. Olive Ridleys and endangered leatherbacks."

"And you moonlight as a machete-wielding maniac, apparently, capturing innocent women off the beach."

Despite the grimness of their situation, the sweat pouring off him and the strain in his muscles as he paddled like hell down the coast, his lips curved at her tart reply.

"You know what they say," he drawled. "It's tough work, but somebody's got to do it."

Chapter 2

"Where are you taking me?"

His hostage's sexy voice cut through the darkness as he power-stroked as hard as he could.

He inhaled raggedly, the muscles in his arms aching from the exertion. He considered himself in pretty darn good shape, but this insane pace and the strain of paddling both of them were definitely taking a toll on him.

Since he didn't have breath to spare, he chose not to answer her question with a long explanation. "We're almost there. See those lights ahead and to the left?"

She looked in the direction he pointed. "Yes," she answered after a moment, wrapping her arms around herself.

She couldn't possibly be cold, could she? he wondered. It was a mild night, probably only low 80s, and slightly cooler out here on the water, but it was far from chilly. Of course, she was only wearing a bikini and she wasn't paddling her guts out.

"That's my research station. Playa Hermosa. I've got a Jeep there."

She shuddered and tightened her arms around herself.

He grimaced, wishing he had time to offer her words of comfort. He wasn't crazy about the idea of traumatizing a bride on her honeymoon, but it couldn't be helped.

He allowed a quick moment to wonder where her groom might be lurking in this miserable drama and why he had left his luscious little wife even for a minute. Maybe out fishing on the missing yacht? The Pacific coast of the Osa Peninsula was rich with marine life, from marlins to sailfish to tuna.

Any groom who would abandon his bride to go fishing deserved to have her kidnapped. Ren certainly wouldn't have let her out of his sight.

Something about Rafferty's next intended victim appealed to him on some deep, visceral level. In the pale moonlight shimmering off the water, she looked lush and soft and delectable, with creamy skin and voluptuous features.

A blond cream puff, Rafferty had called her. Ren had a feeling she wouldn't appreciate the nickname— or his sudden fierce desire to swallow her up in one delicious bite.

The discovery did *not* improve his mood. In two years, he hadn't been able to drum up even a tiny smidgeon of enthusiasm for the whores in the rough and ready town of Puerto Jiménez, no matter how determined their attempts at seduction during his infrequent visits to the cantinas.

In the space of the last hour, he had witnessed a vicious murder, had kidnapped a woman for the first— hopefully *only*—time in his life and terrified her out of her skull, then paddled like hell across the ocean.

Yet here he sat with the biggest hard-on of his life.

Disgusted with himself, Ren growled a fairly vile curse in Spanish and felt like an even bigger pervert when the woman in front of him flinched as if he were planning to ravish her any second now, something he was fairly sure was impossible—not to mention rather ill-advised—in a sea kayak adrift on the open ocean.

He could ignore the heat and hunger. He'd had plenty of practice, after all. Excepting those first wild months after the fire when he hadn't climbed out of a bottle, for two years he had focused his entire energies on his work, leaving no room for anything else.

Though he had the occasional research assistant and used volunteers to help him patrol the beaches for nesting sites, he lived a solitary life for the most part, and that was just the way he liked it. He had a few friends on the Peninsula, but most of the villagers considered him the Crazy Turtle Man of Playa Hermosa.

Early in his time in Costa Rica five years ago, a few heated altercations with poachers after the culinary prize of turtle eggs taken beyond the legal season had started the rumors. His wildness of the last two years had cemented the reputation.

He imagined this little escapade would probably add more fuel to the fire if word got out, which he had no doubt it would.

No help for it, he thought. Snatching Rafferty's

little blond cream puff had been an impulse, but he couldn't regret it.

At least not yet.

When he neared Playa Hermosa, he paddled as far as he could and let the waves push them the rest of the way. Close to shore, he climbed out and pulled the kayak up the beach.

In the moonlight, his hostage looked numb, her features expressionless and dull, and he hoped to hell she wasn't going into some kind of delayed shock and taking a mental vacation on him. That would be just what he needed right about now—a catatonic sexpot in a bikini.

Though he would have liked to consign Rafferty's expensive kayak to the sharks, he couldn't find it in him to waste such a sleek, beautiful craft. With Olivia Lambert still inside, he muscled it up past the high-tide mark, then reached a hand to help her out.

"Here we are. We'll just grab my keys inside and a change of clothes for you and be on our way."

She gazed at him blankly, and he wondered again if she'd lost her marbles somewhere out there on the ocean.

"It's okay," he tried to reassure her.

After a long pause, she slipped her hand in his and climbed out of the kayak as regally as a princess. Her small hand was cool and soft as the petals of the hibiscus and orchids and frangipani flowering around them, and she trembled only a little.

It was dark and would probably begin raining any minute, but for now the moon was full and clearly illuminated the short pathway from the beach to his station. He gestured for her to proceed him.

"Head through those trees right there," he said.

"We're on the only developed road in this area, if you can call the mud track in the green season a road."

He should have been tipped off to her intent, but her abstracted, out-of-it air fooled him. He was completely unprepared when she took just a shuffling step forward in the direction of the trail, then whipped around the other way and took off down the beach.

For about half a second, he was severely tempted to just let her slip away into the jungle. His life and the surreal trip it had become in the last hour would sure be a hell of a lot easier without having to deal with a soft dumpling of a bride who seemed on the verge of dissolving into a quivering mass of fear any second now.

He even took a step toward his research station, then he growled an oath and turned around. He couldn't let her just wander off out here. The jungle was a danger-ous place, especially for a soft thing like her.

She had several seconds head start and she was faster than he would have expected. She was almost to the thick shelter of trees, where he would have a much tougher time catching her.

Out of patience and breath, he finally lunged at her from the side in a classic football tackle his college linebacker of a brother would have been happy with, just before she would have slipped into the brush.

With an oomph, she hit the sand and his momentum carried him on top of her.

For a second, he froze there, some savage male beast inside him taking primitive delight in her soft curves.

He was aroused all over again, he realized with no small measure of disgust.

All his life, he had considered himself a pretty decent guy. His parents taught all three of their sons to treat women with respect and honor, and Ren thought he had completely absorbed those lessons.

So why did this woman—this *situation*—seem to bring out the worst in him and make him feel like some kind of rampaging beast?

She squirmed beneath him, fighting frantically to be free. "Please," she whimpered. "Please don't."

Her words and the panicked fear behind them were like taking a dip in spring runoff back home in Utah. He stood up, this time keeping a close hold on her wrist.

"I'm not going to attack you," he growled, tugging her back up the beach toward the station.

"M-more than you already have?"

"You're alive, aren't you?" he snapped. "At least for now."

Wrong choice of words, he realized, when she hissed in a breath. He was grimly aware she was trembling now as she stumbled along behind him.

He hated her terror and wanted to explain everything but he didn't dare take the time. Rafferty and his men hadn't reached Playa Hermosa yet, but he knew they couldn't be far behind. Her little attempt at escape and the subsequent delay it caused could turn out to be a deadly mistake for both of them.

He could tell her everything as they drove to the little police outpost in Matapalo, but for now they needed to get the hell out of Dodge.

"Look, I'm trying to help you here. You can believe me or not, but there are some mighty nasty creatures stalking the Osa after dark, not a few of them human.

Trust me, sweetheart, right now I'm your best chance of getting out of this whole thing in one piece. If you run away from me again, I'm going to have to tie you up for your own safety and neither of us wants that."

She muttered something under her breath he didn't catch but he didn't have time to waste wondering about it. He just headed up the hillside to the research station, keeping his hand firmly clamped around her wrist the whole way.

He had locked the station to protect his equipment inside when he headed down to Suerte del Mar earlier and his keys were zippered into the same waterproof bag on his kayak, but he quickly found the emergency spare snugged under Yertle, the huge leatherback carved by one of his research assistants the summer before.

With one eye trained on the hill for approaching headlights, he unlocked the door and yanked her inside behind him.

He didn't dare let her go so he kept her wrist firmly in his grasp as he grabbed his Jeep keys, then headed to his bedroom and flipped on the generator-driven light. When she caught sight of his bed, she dug her heels into the concrete floor as if he were going to yank aside the mosquito netting and ravish her on the spot.

He sighed and forced away the annoyance. There was no time for it. If she wanted to think he was some kind of mad rapist, so be it.

Of course, it didn't help that seeing her in the light made him all too aware of her lush, curvy femininity, so blond and soft and different from anything to be found in this wild corner of Costa Rica.

He opened a drawer and grabbed a couple clean T-shirts and some shorts. They would be way too big for her, but they'd have to do.

"Here, put these on," he ordered.

That blank stare was back—he saw it take over the stunning blue of her eyes—and he sighed. She seemed to retreat into some hidden corner of her mind, somewhere he couldn't reach. Right now, he didn't have the time or the patience to try.

"Look, we're in for a wild ride to Matapalo if we want to make it before Rafferty and his goons find us. Unless I miss my guess, we're going to have rain in a few minutes and even with the canvas top on the Jeep, you'll be soaked. You're going to need something else to wear."

This would be a hell of a memory from her honeymoon, he thought, as he finally just grabbed the T-shirt and pulled it over her head. She cooperated enough to push her arms through the sleeves.

If her husband had left her at Rafferty's to go fishing knowing he owed the bastard money, Ren hoped the idiot was impaled by a marlin and then stung by a couple thousand jellyfish.

He grabbed a pair of shorts and yanked them up over her hips. She flinched when he touched the bare skin at her waist.

"If I had evil designs on you, don't you think I'd be taking your clothes off instead of putting more on?" he growled.

That seemed to pierce the haze of panic around her and he watched some of the blankness recede. He didn't have time to be grateful for it as he suddenly remembered one more item that might come in handy. He hurried to his closet and dug for a moment, emerging a moment later with a large shoe box.

In the distance, he thought he heard the throb of an engine and he swore harshly. "Come on. We've got to haul ass."

He half dragged, half carried her to his Jeep and threw her inside, tossing the box and a few other items he'd grabbed on the way out the door into the back seat, alongside the emergency survival pack he always kept there in case he found himself stranded on some remote beach somewhere by weather or tides.

He quickly reached across the seat to buckle her shoulder belt, earning a quick ragged breath for his trouble. As her chest expanded with the sharp inhalation, the movement pressed her voluptuous breasts to his arm and he felt the hairs there rise—along with other parts of him that had no business noticing her in the middle of running for their lives.

He had been too damn long without a woman.

His beat-up old Jeep started immediately—a minor miracle—and he gunned the engine down the rutted, bumpy dirt track.

At least the afternoon rains had dried somewhat so the roads were at least moderately passable for now, until the evening rains hit.

The few roads in this primitive part of Costa Rica were unreliable at best. This was the only route between Puerto Jiménez and Carate, the gateway to Corcovado National Park.

In the relatively dry summer months from December to May, he could usually count on being able to make

it to Jiménez in only an hour, but in the rainy season—
the *green* season, they called it to keep from scaring
away the tourists—when it rained at least an inch or two
every day, it could take him three times as long.

And he usually just counted on being stuck at the
station for the entire month of October, with its near
constant deluge, unless he caught a flight out of the
airstrip at Carate.

Here in late September, he still had a possibility of
making it safely. All he had to do right now was get them
to the small police station in Matapalo. But if the rains
hit while they were en route, this dirt road would
become a slick, dangerous mess.

He just had to hope that didn't happen.

As her captor gunned the rattletrap Jeep's engine and
sped away from his lair with his tires spitting mud and
gravel, Olivia held on to the grab bar and divided her
time between clamping her teeth together to keep from
crying out and whispering a fervent prayer that her
pitiful life would be spared.

She wanted to be numb, to tune it all out. It was
taking every ounce of concentration to keep her
emotions contained.

Instead of the blessed oblivion she would have vastly
preferred, every sense seemed accentuated, as if the
world had suddenly come sharply into focus. She was
acutely aware of each jostling rut in the road, the throb
of the engine, the heavy, humid air pressing down on her.

She was especially aware of the man beside her—his
overwhelming size and strength.

For the last hour since he stepped out of the jungle,

machete in hand, he had been simply a shadowy, threatening hulk of a man. She hadn't caught a clear glimpse of him until he turned on the lights inside his spartan concrete research station.

Though he was no doubt at least six feet tall, he had not been quite as large as her imagination had conjured up, more lean and lithe than she expected.

During that hideous kayak ride as he had swiftly propelled them through the waves, she had tried *not* to look at him. It was the only way she could keep from letting the panic completely overwhelm her.

Her impression then had been only of some dark, terrifying stranger. The light inside his dwelling had revealed a man of extraordinary good looks. Her friends in Fort Worth would have drooled over someone like him, with those chiseled features, the dark, intense eyes, full mouth, and eyelashes so long they looked fake.

He looked nothing like any scientist she had ever seen. He looked more like some kind of Latino pop star, and she could easily imagine him on a stage somewhere crooning to thousands of screaming girls.

She wasn't at all reassured that he wasn't the hideous monster her imagination had conjured up. Somehow this man seemed far more dangerous to her peace of mind.

He was wild and rugged and beautiful, just like this isolated part of the world, completely out of her realm of experience.

Ren Galvez was exactly the kind of man she would have avoided in Dallas, someone strong and masculine and…and *sensual*.

She caught the word and grimaced at herself. What

did she know if the man was sensual or not? Most likely, he was cold and analytical, more interested in facts than figures, at least the feminine kind.

But there had been that moment back on the beach when he had tackled her and his hard, muscled body had pressed her into the sand. Through her fear and the adrenaline pumping violently through her system as she tried to escape, she could swear she had detected definite interest from the man.

She thought for certain he would attack her there, press his obvious advantage in size and strength to over-power her. Instead, he had helped her to her feet and guided her to his utilitarian quarters, where he had proceeded to find clothes for her.

What on earth did he want with her? He continued to assure her he wouldn't hurt her, but if rape wasn't on his mind, what other motive could he have?

Was he after money? He had asked her name but maybe that was only to reassure himself he'd snatched the right heiress.

She had heard about prevalent ransom kidnappings in some Central and South American countries, but everything she had read about Costa Rica assured her the country was safe. Ticos were proud of their stable government and their relative prosperity, and the country went out of its way to eagerly welcome visitors.

Her imagination buzzed with possibilities. He said he was a scientist. The equipment in his dwelling certainly backed up the assertion. There had been that carved turtle on the porch and the sign over the door that said Playa Hermosa Turtle Institute.

Maybe he was looking for funding and had hit on a

rather unorthodox method of raising support. It seemed ludicrous in the extreme, but for the life of her, she couldn't come up with any other explanation.

Why else would a turtle researcher snatch a guest from a neighboring estate, just to rush off through the night with her?

It all seemed so surreal. Things like this—mysterious strangers grabbing her at machete-point—didn't happen to her.

Everything about this situation terrified her. Most of all, she hated not knowing what was happening and Ren Galvez—if that was his real name—seemed in no hurry to explain.

She desperately wanted to trust him when he said he wouldn't hurt her. But then again, she had a lousy habit of fooling herself into believing the best in people.

Just look at her choice of erstwhile fiancés. For six months, she had convinced herself Bradley loved her. How many warning signs had she ignored, just to avoid stirring up the waters?

She had been so caught up in the unaccustomed sensation of pleasing her father, for once, that Bradley and her misgivings about him had almost seemed superfluous.

Not that any of that mattered right now while she was in the hands of a madman who was going to drive them both over a cliff into the Pacific. She swallowed a scream as the Jeep slid toward the edge, but her captor yanked it back to the middle of the track that passed for a road.

Her heart was still pounding when the sky unleashed the nightly rains he warned about.

Rain seemed like such a benign term for this. Growing up in Texas, she thought she knew about precipitation, but this was like nothing in her experience. It was as if someone had suddenly turned on a hot high-pressure shower and let it loose on the countryside.

Buckets of water gushed off the trees and cascaded down the road. The canvas roof of the Jeep offered some protection but not much. In only a few moments, Olivia was soaked.

The Jeep slid again, moving inexorably toward the side. This time she didn't bother to contain her scream.

"I've got it," he assured her. "Hang on."

He muscled out of the skid, then downshifted for the next hill. She didn't know how he managed it—years of experience, probably—but he managed to get them up the next hill, and they plowed through mud and muck and rivers of rain rushing down the road.

As abruptly as it started, the rain ceased, as if someone turned off that imaginary tap somewhere.

She thought she saw lights ahead and the impression was verified a moment later when he pulled up to a small cluster of buildings—two or three with what looked like a small general store and a couple of ramshackle houses.

He parked in front of the store, where Olivia was surprised to see a sign tacked to the window of the little storefront that said *Policía*. An odd destination for a would-be rapist, she had to admit, and found some degree of comfort from that.

Galvez turned off the engine. "This won't take long. In a minute, this will all be over and you'll be safe, I promise."

Hope and confusion warring within her, Olivia watched him open his door and start to climb out.

And then the shooting started.

Chapter 3

For half a second, Olivia wasn't sure what was happening. It sounded like firecrackers going off somewhere or a car backfiring, but then she hadn't seen any other vehicles on the road.

Before the reality had really soaked in that those were bullets flying around, her captor suddenly leaped back into the Jeep and started the vehicle's engine.

"Get down," he yelled, driving with one hand and reaching the other across the Jeep to shove her head to her knees when she only stared blankly at him.

The Jeep slithered in the slick mud, then the rear wheels engaged. She heard a ping ricochet off the metal skin as bullets continued to rain around them. Miraculously, none hit the tires. A blowout in these conditions would be disastrous, she knew.

She huddled there, her hands over her head, numb

with fear and certain that any moment now, Galvez could take a hit and the vehicle would go careening out of control.

Her breathing hitched and she fought hysteria, wanting nothing so much as to curl into the fetal position and disappear. She heard sirens behind them and could see the strobe of lights piercing the darkness as the Jeep rattled and shook its way down the trail.

She didn't know how close the pursuers were—and she wasn't completely sure whether she wanted to evade them or have them catch up. She wanted out of this situation *now* and at this point she was willing to take any rescue offered.

On the other hand, she wasn't sure she was really crazy about turning herself over to police officers so willing to shoot first and ask questions later. They didn't seem particularly concerned about her safety while they fired a barrage of bullets at the Jeep.

"Hang on," Galvez ordered.

As if she could do anything else, besides pray. She gripped the roll bar with one hand and braced one hand against the dashboard to steady herself against the wild jostling of the vehicle.

"What are you doing?!" she gasped when he suddenly turned off the headlights, pitching them into darkness.

"Trust me," he said.

Before she could tell him how absolutely ludicrous such a statement was under the circumstances, he jerked the wheel off the road into what looked like impenetrable jungle. There must be some kind of track here, but for the life of her, she couldn't see anything. How did he know where he was going? she wondered, as rain-soaked branches whipped the Jeep.

At least the shooting stopped, but she fully expected them to ram headlong into a tree any moment now. Some moonlight filtered through the thick trees, but he couldn't possibly see more than a few feet in front of them.

She was not cut out for wild moonlit rides through the rain forest. She had been known to have panic attacks in rush hour traffic, for heaven's sake.

After several heart-pounding moments—each one that seemed to last a lifetime—he turned the Jeep again, this time driving over plants and around trees until they were off even that narrow track, swallowed up by the rain forest.

He shut off the engine and turned to face her, and she saw the gleam of his teeth in the pale moonlight.

"End of the road, sweetheart. I think we lost them for now." He climbed out of the Jeep and reached behind the seat for a backpack.

She gazed blankly at him. "You're…you're just going to leave me here?"

He gave a short laugh. "Do you want me to?"

Some creature screeched in the night and Olivia shivered. She wanted to think she could find her way back to the main road, but she wasn't completely certain.

The alternative—huddling here all night on the off chance that someone might come along and find her—was not at all appealing.

"What's happening?" She hated the thin note of panic in her voice but seemed unable to keep it at bay. "Why were the police shooting at us back there?"

He pulled a few more items out of the back of the Jeep and set them on the ground, then opened her door and reached a hand to help her out—or rather, he didn't really give her a choice in the matter, just tugged her out of the vehicle.

He had his machete out again, she saw with a spurt of fear. But as soon as she climbed down from the high-profile vehicle, he turned around and started scything away at the underbrush.

"My fault," he finally answered, dragging several of the branches he cut over the Jeep. "I should have taken into consideration that Rafferty probably owns every officer of the law between here and Puerto Jiménez. There's only one halfway decent road around the Peninsula to the Golfo Dulce and the bastard has probably already got roadblocks all along the way."

He was trying to conceal the vehicle from their pursuers, she finally realized as he continued to cut branches and huge, leafy ferns. She stood with her arms wrapped around her, watching him work.

"I guess Rafferty and your groom—what's his name?"

For a moment, she couldn't think how to answer him. "Uh, Bradley," she finally said.

"Right. Bradley." He said the name with thinly veiled scorn. "I guess Jimbo and Bradley aren't going to let me just run off with you after all."

"Did you really think they would?"

"I wasn't thinking, if you want the truth. If I had been, I would have realized that with one phone call, Rafferty has probably got his people up and down the whole damn coast, all the way to Jiménez, roadblocks in every one-donkey town from Agua Buena to Plataneres. He's probably told the rural police some cock-and-bull story, all about how I stormed onto Suerte del Mar and kidnapped one of his guests."

"The nerve of the man."

Her sarcasm came out of nowhere, surprising the heck out of her. In the moonlight, she saw his teeth widen into an appreciative grin. She blamed her sudden breathlessness on the lingering adrenaline buzz.

"Exactly," he said. "I am *not* going to let the bastard pin this on me. He knows exactly why I rescued you from Suerte del Mar, but you can bet the house he's not going to share that bit of information with the *policía*."

Rescued? Is that what he called scaring the life out of her, dragging her down the beach at machete-point and paddling her across the open ocean with sharks circling them?

"The chief of police in Puerto Jiménez and I go way back," he went on.

Somehow she didn't find it surprising that this man had had brushes with the law before, given his criminal record so far. Ren Galvez's name was probably engraved on a cell somewhere, at the very least.

"He's a good man, a rare breed among officials down here who can't be bribed. If we can make it there, I know I can convince Mañuel Solera of what really happened."

He smiled again, looking entirely too cheerful under the circumstances. "Good thing I brought you some decent shoes."

He rummaged through a box and held up a pair of hiking boots.

The sight of them filled her with dread. "Uh, why do I need decent shoes?"

"There's a trail through the Gulfo Dulce Forest Reserve to El Tigre. We can hook up with it back on the track we were just on. The good news is, it's only ten miles or so. Once in El Tigre, we can catch a ride into Jiménez."

She did not like the sound of this. Ten miles or so? He couldn't be serious. He couldn't really expect her to *walk* ten miles through the jungle, could he?

"Um, I'm not much of a hiker. I should probably tell you that up front. You're obviously in a hurry and I'm afraid I'll only slow you down. Why don't you just go on ahead? I'm sure I can find my way back to the road."

Maybe.

"Nice try. Trust me, sweetheart. You *don't* want to wait for Rafferty to find you. He won't be in a pleasant mood."

If they were going to talk about moods, she was pretty certain she had James Rafferty beat when it came to lousy ones right about now. She was tired and scared and hadn't eaten in about seven hours.

The jungle around them teemed with life, buzzing insects and the flap of fruit bats overhead. She heard a rustle in the bushes of some unseen creature, then a terrifying, low-throated yowl from what sounded like only a few yards away.

She gasped and grabbed for him in the darkness, grabbing hold of his shirt and a good portion of warm skin. When faced with the alternatives, a delusional man with a machete didn't seem like such a bad bet.

"What was that?" she gasped.

He shrugged and she felt his muscles ripple. "Sounded like a puma. They're pretty common out here. He's farther away than he sounded, though. And he probably won't bother us."

Probably was not exactly reassuring.

"If you're talking mammals, it's not the big cats you

should worry about so much out here as the white-lipped peccaries."

"P-peccaries?" She realized she was still clinging to his arm and quickly released him. Immediately, she felt chilled, even though the air was still heavy and warm.

She had seen a small herd of wild peccaries once while visiting her grandmother in south Texas and had no desire to bump into any out here in the dark.

"It's not uncommon to see a herd of twenty or more out here. Don't worry, though. You'll smell them and hear the cracking of their teeth long before you see them. Once you hear them, all you have to do to get away is climb a tree."

She swallowed a sob. She *so* didn't want to be here. She wanted to be safe and dry and blessedly cool in Fort Worth in her condo, even if that meant she had to deal with all the wedding gifts that needed to be returned and hear a dozen messages from her father on her answering machine trying to change her mind.

Sometimes you've got to just play the cards you're dealt, sugar. She could hear her maternal grandmother's drawl in her ear and knew Belinda was right. She didn't have a lot of choices. At the moment, this man didn't seem inclined to hurt her and had actually gone out of his way to be solicitous. Though it seemed insane, she was going to have to trust him, at least until she could figure out a way out of this mess.

"Sit down and let's change your shoes. You're going to have to wear a pair of my socks. Sorry about that."

He pulled out a flashlight and a moment later a beam of light shone into his pack. He dug around for a moment, then produced a pair of thick socks. "Hurry.

We don't have much time," he said as he handed them to her, then pulled a pair of hiking boots from the box he'd thrown into the Jeep at the last moment.

She leaned against a tree trunk and hurriedly pulled them on, wincing a little at the pinch of wearing someone else's shoes. Surely not his. They were far too small, most definitely made for a woman's foot.

It seemed an odd, almost ominous sign to her. Why would he have a pair of women's hiking boots when she'd seen no signs of anyone female living at his abode?

Maybe he was some kind of crazed serial killer who dressed his victims in hiking boots and marched them into the rain forest.

She cursed herself for her vivid imagination. That's what came from watching too many crime dramas on TV.

When the boots were laced, he reached a hand to help her from the trunk.

"Sweet thing like you is going to be eaten alive out here," he murmured, standing entirely too close. Her pulse cranked up a notch. Here was the part where she should probably decide she would rather risk the jungle than whatever grisly fate he had in store for her, but somehow she couldn't make her legs cooperate.

She held her breath, praying he couldn't hear the harsh pounding of her heart. A moment later, she winced at her foolishness as he doused her with bug spray. "That's going to wear off in an hour, so remind me to spray you again."

Without another word, he shouldered his backpack, aimed his flashlight into the thick vegetation, and headed off without looking back to see if she followed.

She could escape right now, just turn around and

race through the trees until she was out of his sight. She could try to find her way back to the main road and take her chances with Rafferty's mood.

Or she could stay here and let the pumas and the jaguars and the white-lipped peccaries get her.

Torn, her insides churning with indecision, she froze. Finally, he must have clued in that she wasn't behind him. He stopped and aimed his flashlight at her. "Come on. We've got a long walk ahead of us, but with any luck you'll be on a plane back to the States by this time tomorrow."

He could have just been telling her what he thought she wanted to hear. A madman would have no reason to tell the truth. Though she warned herself to be cautious, she still found great comfort in his words.

With a long, resigned sigh, she followed him, feeling as if she were leaving more of her common sense behind with every step she took in the unfamiliar boots.

Though it was full dark and had to be past nine o'clock at night by now, the heat still weighed heavily on her. It pressed against her in every direction until she felt as if she were walking through hot gelatin. The trail was muddy from the rains earlier—the *constant* rains, apparently—and soon the mysterious new boots were caked in it. With every step, more mud clung to the boots until she felt as if she were lifting half the trail as she stepped.

After only a few minutes, she was drenched in sweat and wholly miserable. She couldn't see anything but the mud in front of his flashlight beam as it cut through the darkness.

"I hesitate to point this out," she said, "but all the guidebooks say it's not wise to be in the jungle after dark."

"That's what they say."

"Yet here we are."

He aimed his flashlight toward her and in the reflected light, she saw his mouth lifted into a half smile. "You have any better suggestion? Maybe a float plane stashed somewhere I don't know about?"

"Of course not."

"Neither do I. We could kayak around the peninsula, but that would take much longer and would be far more dangerous in the dark. Rafferty's got a power yacht that can move a whole hell of a lot faster than I can paddle. He can patrol the whole coast looking for us and there's nowhere to hide out on the open water. So unless you can come up with some other option, as far as I can tell, we don't have any other choice but to keep walking."

Apparently, Ren Galvez wasn't of the curl-up-right-here-and-die school of thought. She sighed and kept walking.

She never knew it was possible to hate someone with such a fierce, all-consuming passion.

She had been angry with Bradley for his gross betrayal, devastated by her father's complete lack of filial support, hurt at her friends and coworkers for whispering about her behind her back, for acting as if she were the crazy one to get so bent out of shape over a little infidelity before any vows had been spoken.

But she never knew what it meant to *loathe* someone until just this moment. She decided she despised Lorenzo Galvez, with every aching, exhausted, itchy cell of her being.

She hated him. She hated *this*. She was tired, she was

hungry, her feet ached from boots that were too tight and her thighs burned from hiking uphill through the mud.

After perhaps an hour—or two or three or ten, she was too numb to really know for sure—he stopped abruptly. She was so focused on plodding forward, lost in her trance of misery, that she wasn't aware he had planted his feet on the trail until she plowed into him.

He turned and steadied her to keep her from toppling over. "Easy there, sweetheart. Need a drink?"

The air was so humid she felt as if she could swallow it every time she opened her mouth, but at his words, she became aware of a fierce thirst. She had to admit, a big, icy piña colada would be delicious right about now. Instead, she apparently had to settle for the water bottle he pulled out of his pack.

She had a sudden violent urge to bash him over the head with it. Instead, she inhaled a deep, calming yoga breath—the only thing that had sustained her thus far on this hellish journey—and grabbed the bottle from him.

She wanted nothing more than to slump against the nearest tree and collapse, but fear of scorpions or fire ants or any of the other creepy crawlies she'd read about in the guidebooks kept her upright.

Hydrating her system helped allay the worst of her homicidal urges. She still didn't feel exactly favorable toward the man, but at least the impulse to see if she could gouge his eyes out with the mouth of the water bottle seemed to fade.

"We've got to keep moving," he said after only a moment or two.

She drew in a shaky breath, pouring all her energy into keeping her sobs at bay. Just the thought of trying to lift her muck-laden shoes another step felt over-whelming, impossible.

"I can't," she moaned.

"You have to. Just another mile and then we can take a rest, Mrs. Lambert."

She ground her teeth, absurdly infuriated by the address, as if that were the least of his offenses toward her. "Olivia," she snapped.

"Olivia."

He stepped closer, and in the darkness, he seemed like some terrifying, nebulous creature. Still, she could feel the heat emanating from his skin, the energy that surrounded him.

"Close your eyes," he ordered.

"Why?" she asked warily.

"Bug juice. Time for a refresher."

She complied, wishing she could keep her eyes closed and just block this entire ordeal out. She felt vulnerable, exposed, as he moved around her with the deet. She was oddly aware of him, her subconscious registering his location in space every second, even with her eyes closed.

How was it possible for her to be so physically aware of him and yet to fear and despise him at the same time?

She had to be sick and twisted, in addition to this amazingly violent streak she was only just discovering.

"You've been great so far. Twenty more minutes, okay?"

One or both of them would be dead by then, she was fairly certain. If the miserable conditions and the myriad dangers out here didn't kill them, she would do the job herself.

He started off down the trail, just expecting her to blindly follow along, but somehow she couldn't make her legs cooperate. She stood helplessly watching after him as the light disappeared.

The light was back in just a few seconds, with Ren looking disgruntled and frustrated at the end of it. "I know you're worn out, but I'm afraid it's going to rain again soon and we can't stay out here without any kind of shelter. You've got to press forward a little farther. I don't think I can carry both you and the pack for a mile."

Okay, she *really* loathed him now. Yeah, maybe she'd had an extra roll or two for lunch. But where would she be now without those extra few carbs?

"I'm coming," she snapped.

He gave her an encouraging smile that made her want to deck him and then he took off again up the trail.

As she slogged along behind him, she entertained herself with the various revenge scenarios she would enjoy enacting when this was all over. Something involving fire ants and a gallon of honey topped the list, though covering him with truffles and staking him in the middle of a rampaging herd of peccaries came in a close second.

She didn't understand any of this and he didn't seem in a big hurry to explain but somehow as time ticked on, she became less and less convinced he would hurt her.

Whether *she* was going to hurt him was another question entirely, but he seemed genuinely concerned for her safety.

She was certain it was longer than a mile—it had to be three or four, at the least—but he finally stopped.

"Here we go. We can rest here for a few hours, catch some sleep, get something to eat."

She looked around, wondering just how well-camouflaged the shelter must be. She couldn't see anything but trees and understory, even with his high-powered flashlight. It looked no different from the acres of forest they had already trudged around.

"Where?" she asked.

He pointed his flashlight up and for the first time she saw small handholds in the massive trunk of a giant tree, extending farther than the reach of the flashlight beam.

She hitched in a breath as cold fear washed over her like an arctic tide. She had survived having a machete held to her back, being a midnight snack for every insect for miles around and walking through the terrifying jungle. But this was beyond her.

"No. Absolutely not."

"It's not hard, I swear. Okay, a little trickier at night than it would be in the daylight, but we'll be tethered together and I'll be right behind you the whole way. You'll be just fine."

"I know. I'll be just fine down here on solid ground because I am *not* climbing up there. You can't make me."

She didn't care how childish she sounded. Climbing a gigantic tree was *not* in the tour description here.

"Did I mention the mosquito netting? And it's about fifteen degrees cooler up in the canopy. Come on, Olivia. I won't let you fall."

Peccaries weren't good enough. How about fire ants *and* peccaries *and* a couple dozen starving pumas?

"No. No way."

She almost thought she could hear his teeth grinding from here. "Do I have to remind you about the machete?" he asked in an out-of-patience kind of voice.

She crossed her arms across her chest. She wasn't afraid of him anymore, she decided. There simply wasn't room for fear around the loathing.

"Go ahead. Break out your machete. Cut off an arm or two. What's the difference? At least without arms, you can't make me climb and I'd rather bleed to death than go up there."

He gave a short laugh, then clipped it off midway through.

"Hold still," he uttered suddenly, his voice barely a hush amid the whirs and peeps and calls of the rain forest at night.

He whipped his machete out and advanced slowly on her and her breath caught. Maybe he wasn't quite as harmless as she wanted to believe.

"Okay, okay," she squeaked out. "I was bluffing. I'll climb."

"Don't move," he growled. An instant later—before she could even take take another breath—the machete flashed through the night and struck the ground inches from her feet. A shaft of moonlight piercing the canopy gave just enough light for her to see a vine writhing at her feet.

Not a vine, of course. A snake.

Her insides churned and if she'd had anything in her stomach, she was fairly certain she would have lost it right then.

He held out his flashlight and shined it on the headless, still moving snake with a curiously beautiful geometric pattern along its skin. "There you go. Fer-de-lance. The deadliest snake around. A hundred people a year are killed by them in Costa Rica."

She was going to hyperventilate now for sure. She

couldn't seem to catch her breath and the world seemed to spin alarmingly. She drew in a cleansing breath, then another and another until the moist, oxygen-rich air loosened the gnarled tendrils of panic.

"Up in the canopy is just about the only place we can rest without having to worry about them. But it's your choice."

What kind of man was Ren Galvez that he could kill a deadly snake without even breaking a sweat? He had probably just saved her life and he didn't appear to be fazed one iota.

She looked at the terrifying tree trunk, then back at the now blessedly still creature. She swallowed a whimper and straightened her shoulders.

"I'll climb," she said.

Chapter 4

She climbed until her arms were trembling with fatigue and her stomach was a hard knot of nausea. She didn't even want to *think* about the journey back down.

The entire time she climbed, she was aware of him below her and the thin rope tethering them together. He had pulled it from his magic pack that apparently contained everything a person might need to survive in the rain forest in the middle of a nightmare.

She was tied to him, and his harness had a clip attached to the ladder bolted into the trunk. If either of them fell, theoretically the clip would keep them anchored to the tree.

She didn't want to put that theory to the test anytime soon.

She could only concentrate on pulling hand over hand up the ladder, hoping his flashlight beam was aimed somewhere high above her and not at her chunky butt.

At last she reached the last rung on the ladder, just when she was beginning to think this whole thing would be easier if she just begged him to slice through her tether with his machete and let her tumble a hundred feet to the jungle floor.

"Great. Over you go. Good job."

Though she was severely tempted to kick him right in his cheery little teeth, she didn't have any energy to spare for the task. Instead, she pulled herself onto a swaying wood platform, perhaps eight feet in circumference, then spiderwalked to the trunk in the middle and flopped to her stomach, breathing hard and hanging on to the massive trunk with all her might.

He followed her up, pulling off his pack and stretching his shoulders. "Don't like heights much, do you?"

"You could say that."

She didn't think he was interested in the root of her fear. During her first year of boarding school when she was eight, two of the older girls coaxed her onto the roof with promises to show her their secret clubhouse and then locked her there, clinging to a gargoyle for three terrifying hours until the headmistress found her well after dark.

That childhood trauma three stories up seemed like a walk in the park compared to this.

"I'm sorry to put you through this," he said.

Oddly, she thought he meant it. His concern slid through her, warming the chilled corners of her psyche, until she sternly reminded herself he was the one posing a danger to her.

"You're safe up here. See, there's a railing all the way around and I can even close off the opening we climbed through so you don't have to worry about stumbling off in the dark."

As if she needed that image in her head, too.

"Great," she mumbled.

"We'll have a gorgeous view in the morning."

She declined comment on that, quite certain daylight would only accentuate just how high up they were.

He sat down across from her and dug around in his pack. A moment later, he pulled out a lantern.

"I thought I had this in here," he said. "Can you hold the flashlight for a minute?"

She complied and watched as he lit the mantles. A moment later, the lantern buzzed on, illuminating their perch far better than the weak light of the flashlight.

While she still clung to the trunk, he moved around the platform, pulling down and securing mosquito netting that had been rolled up and tied to the over-hanging roof.

It made a cozy, almost intimate shelter.

"What is this place?" she asked.

"Research station. Not mine. There aren't too many sea turtles in the rain forest canopy."

His teeth flashed in the lantern light and she almost smiled back in reflex, then caught herself and jerked her features back into a cool expression.

"A friend of mine is studying rain forest bromeliads. Plants that grow without soil, capturing rainfall and drawing nourishment from the air," he explained, much to her relief.

She'd had no idea what bromeliads might be—they sounded like nasty camel-shaped bugs—and she was very grateful she didn't have to reveal her ignorance.

"Her study grant ran out a few months ago," Ren went on, "but she hopes to be back at the end of the rainy season."

As if on cue, the downpour started again, rattling against the wooden roof of their lofty shelter. There was no buildup to the rain here, she had discovered. One moment it was dry, the next the clouds let loose with a mighty torrent.

She listened to the loud music of the rain, unlike anything she'd ever experienced before. It was a symphony of sound, the percussive clatter hitting the roof, the splat of hard drops bouncing off leaves, the low rumble of a distant river somewhere.

And the smell. It was wild and dramatic, like earth and growth and *life*.

She wasn't much of a gardener, though she did grow a few vegetables and some herbs for cooking in containers in the small backyard of her condo. She loved the scent and feel of dirt under her fingertips. This was the same kind of smell, only on killer steroids.

She couldn't say she found it unappealing, just *overwhelming*.

She couldn't help comparing it to gentle summer rain in Texas, with the sweet, clean scent of wet pavement and wet grass.

She couldn't imagine any two more different experiences from the same act of nature.

She wanted to go home.

The sudden fierce craving for the familiar was so overwhelming she couldn't seem to breathe around it. She wanted to be sitting on her tiny covered patio, with barely room for one lawn chair, listening to the wind sigh in the oak tree and her neighbor's TV playing too loudly.

She wanted the safety and familiarity of her normal routine, the comfort of things she had always taken for granted—electric lights and TiVo and warm running water.

Would she ever see her condo again? Her father? Her girlfriends? She shivered, unable to bear the idea of dying, trapped in the middle of such *foreignness*.

"You're not cold, are you?"

He had been right. It was much cooler up here than down in the murky soup of the understory, but she was still warm. She shook her head, trying hard to forget they were dozens of feet in the air.

"I'm okay."

"I've got some MREs in my pack. You need to eat something."

She nodded, though for all her hunger of before, she wasn't completely sure she could swallow anything with this ball of dread in her stomach.

"You have everything in there, apparently."

"Pays to be prepared. I've got enough supplies for three or four days on my own in here, so we should be fine until tomorrow afternoon. I've been stranded by washed-out bridges or bad roads a few times and having an emergency pack has come in very handy. I keep one in my Jeep and one in the kayak, just in case."

His way of life was as foreign to her as this monsoon rain. She couldn't fathom needing to live off her wits for days at a time.

"While we're up here, you might want to take your boots and socks off to give your feet a chance to dry out a little. Foot rot is a big problem when you're hiking in the tropics."

Lovely. Just what she needed. While he pulled a couple of brown-packaged meals out of his pack and started to open them, she unlaced the borrowed boots and slid them off, wincing as fire scorched along her nerve endings.

"What's the matter?" he asked.

"Blisters."

He dropped the MREs. "Let me take a look."

She didn't want him coming any closer. She was shaky and off balance enough up here in their aerie.

"That's not necessary," she mumbled. "I just need a bandage."

He frowned, ignoring her protest as he approached with the lantern. She felt supremely self-conscious as he knelt in front of her and reached for her still stocking-clad foot.

He held her foot up to the light and hissed out a curse when he saw her socks were pink with blood at the heel and the widest part of her foot.

"Why didn't you say something?" he asked sharply.

"I believe I told you several times I wanted to stay put."

"You didn't tell me I was turning your feet into bloody stumps!"

If she didn't know he was a soulless monster, she would almost have thought he sounded guilty.

"I've got a well-stocked first aid kit in my bag. Let's put some salve on. Hang on."

She decided to take his words literally and continued to cling tightly to the massive trunk of the tree, listening to the rain pound the roof while he found what he needed.

She expected him to simply hand her the ointment

and bandages for her blisters. Instead, he sat on the floor in front of her and picked up her foot again. His hands were warm, his skin calloused, but sensations rippled through her at his touch.

What on earth was *wrong* with her? The man had kidnapped her, for heaven's sake. This would be a good time for her to kick him right over the side.

Even as she thought the impulse, she knew she wouldn't. For one thing, she wasn't sure she could climb back down by herself.

Instead, she sat motionless, doing her best to keep from trembling as he touched her. It was fear, she told herself, but the assertion rang hollow.

In the lantern light, he looked mysterious and dark, all sharp angles and lean curves. He was extraordinarily handsome, she thought again. He didn't at all fit her image of someone who would devote his life to science and the study of turtles.

She might have suspected him of lying if she hadn't seen his research station firsthand, with all the gadgets and gizmos.

She supposed he could be a CIA agent or something, using turtle research as his cover. It was far easier to believe.

His fingers moved with surprising tenderness as he rubbed salve on her skin. Her feet had always been sensitive and his touch felt incredibly soothing after the exertion of the last few hours. She couldn't seem to control another shiver.

He mistook her reaction for pain. "I'm sorry to have to hurt you more," he said. "By tomorrow you'll be safe and sound in Puerto Jiménez."

She flexed her toes as he stuck on a bandage. "So you say."

"I swear it, Olivia. It should only take us four or five hours to hike to El Tigre, and it should be easy to catch a ride from there to Port J on the *colectivo*, which is kind of like a bus."

Five more hours of hiking. She wasn't sure she could bear even ten more minutes. She said nothing, though, and he finished bandaging her feet in silence. When he was done, he moved back to the MREs. She watched him put a tray that looked like a TV dinner in a small green bag. He then poured water from a water bottle in with it.

He repeated the actions with a second MRE, then set them both propped up against the railing at an angle.

Finally, she had to ask, though she wanted to pretend none of this was happening and she was just waiting for a table at The Mansion on Turtle Creek back in Dallas. "What are you doing?"

"Heating our dinner. MREs come with a heating element. You activate it with water. Believe it or not, it makes a pretty decent meal. There are some crackers and raisins in the bag. You can eat those while we wait."

She had to admit, the food tasted delicious, for something that had been shoved in the bottom of a backpack for heaven knows how long. When the entrées were done, he handed her one. The roast beef and mashed potatoes weren't gourmet cuisine, by any stretch of the imagination, but she could see how the meals could sustain fighting men in the field.

If she concentrated with all her might, she could almost forget she was eating it dozens of feet up in the air.

"Your husband must be worried sick about you."

She made a noncommittal sound, fiercely hoping he would let the topic rest.

She should have known better. Like everything else in this miserable evening, luck was not on her side.

"You can call him from the police station in Puerto Jiménez tomorrow to let him know you're safe."

"Am I?"

He sighed. "I know you don't believe me, but you're far better off here than back at Suerte del Mar."

She set down her plastic fork and regarded him in the flickering lantern light. "You keep saying that. But I felt perfectly safe until you came along, Mr. Galvez. In the twenty-four hours I was there, nobody else pulled a machete on me or dragged me up a mountainside or made me climb a thousand feet up in the air. You're the only one who appears to pose a threat to me."

"If I had left you there with Rafferty, your perception might be entirely different."

"What did James Rafferty ever do to you that would make you so desperate or angry or whatever it is that you had to kidnap a guest of his, an innocent woman, and drag me through all this?"

He set his tray aside and studied her for a long moment. She knew she must look horrific, bedraggled and sticky, with her hair going in a hundred directions. She had to wonder what he saw on her features.

She knew she had none of her mother's lush beauty, the sex appeal that had drawn a shrewd, hardened businessman like Wallace Lambert to woo and marry a stripper he met in a Dallas bar.

She had her mother's figure, but on Olivia, it looked dumpy, bordering on chubby. And her face had none of Maelene's radiance that came through clearly in all the photographs Olivia had seen of the mother she couldn't remember.

For the first time in years, she wished it were otherwise. What was the value in having a stripper for a mother when she didn't have the first idea how to hootchy-kootchy?

"You first," he finally said. "Why, of all the possible destinations on earth, were you honeymooning on Suerte Del Mar?"

She frowned, ignoring the niggle of guilt that she hadn't told him the truth. For heaven's sake, she thought. He kidnapped her. Why did she feel as if she had to share her life story with the man?

"James Rafferty invited us," she finally said.

"I asked you before but you didn't answer. How much money does your husband owe Rafferty?"

"Nothing," she mumbled, which was technically true since she didn't *have* a husband.

She was a lousy liar. She had been ever since childhood, when she used to hem and haw and blush fiery red whenever she tried to get a falsehood past her father.

She could only be glad it was dark and he had turned down the lantern to conserve fuel. She had absolutely no poker face and was lousy in any game of chance.

Bradley hadn't been, she remembered. He lived for his weekly high-stakes poker game with his stockbroker and a few other Dallas-area movers and shakers.

Could he have been caught up in online casinos such as Rafferty's highly successful operations?

"Has he had any other business dealings with Rafferty?" Galvez asked her. "Investments that might have gone sour, that kind of thing?"

"No. As far as I know, they met through mutual friends."

"Rafferty doesn't have any friends," he said flatly. "Nor is he the sort to do magnanimous favors like inviting newlyweds to honeymoon at his Costa Rican villa just for the hell of it."

"You know him so well?"

"No, I don't think anybody really knows the man. But we've been neighbors for several years and I've learned a few things in that time. And more tonight than I ever wanted to know."

Questions crowded through her mind. Perhaps at last she would find some answers to a few of them.

"What did you learn tonight?"

He looked for a moment as if he would answer her, but he changed the subject instead. "Where was your husband when I found you on the beach trail?"

She didn't have a husband. But her unlamented ex-fiancé was probably at home playing naked Twister with his personal assistant. "Um, I don't know," she answered, again telling the truth as far as she could.

"What does he do for a living?"

She bristled at the interrogation. "I'm not telling you another thing about…about *anything* until you give me some information in return. What is this all about? Why do you think I'm in danger from James Rafferty? I'm nothing to him. Less than nothing! I've never even met the man."

"But your husband has, and that's the important thing."

A strange, unearthly cry echoed through the night and she shivered again, pulling her knees up and wrapping her arms around them. Peccaries couldn't climb, but what about jaguars or pumas? And were any monkey species around here carnivores? She wasn't sure she wanted to ask.

"From everything I've heard about Rafferty, he gives millions away to charity and has personally revitalized the economy of this area with his ecotourist resorts. He's considered quite an environmentalist. I would think a biologist like you would have nothing but praise for the man. What could you possibly have against him?"

He shrugged, looking suddenly hard and dangerous. "Call me old-fashioned, but it kind of pisses me off to watch him murder a woman in cold blood over her sugar daddy's gambling debts."

She gasped. "You're making that up."

"Am I?"

He had to be. That sort of thing just didn't happen among civilized people. Rafferty had been written up in a dozen financial magazines for his success in business and for his philanthropic efforts. Bradley had showed her a few during their engagement.

"I wish I could agree with you and say this is all some kind of horrible mistake. But it's true. I saw it. Why do you think his goons were chasing me? Why were the police shooting at us? Not for the hell of it. Because Rafferty is trying to shut me up—and you, by default."

"Me? I didn't do anything! If what you say is true, why did you have to drag me into this?"

He sighed. "Five minutes before I bumped into you on the trail, I watched your benevolent philanthropist shoot a bullet into the brain of a woman at his pool, then taunt the woman's lover about how his wife and kids would be next unless he paid what he owed. I saw the whole damn thing and Rafferty knows it. That's why he wants me dead and why I had to get the hell out of Dodge."

"None of which explains why you decided to take me along for the ride!"

He studied her in the darkness, the silence broken by the steady rain plopping against the leaves around them.

"As Rafferty was standing over the body of the woman he had just killed, he made reference to you. Or at least to a blond cream puff he planned for his next course. I'm assuming he meant you."

Cream puff? Rafferty had called her a *cream puff?* She flushed. Okay, so she had a little more than the average woman up top and her hips were unfortunately on the bimboesque side, but that didn't make her a cream puff, for heaven's sake.

Is that the way *Galvez* looked at her as well?

"I think Rafferty planned to use you to enforce your husband's gambling debts in some way. Since I had just witnessed his particular form of debt collection, when I bumped into you, I assumed the worst."

"You think he planned to kill me too?"

"Or hurt you somehow until your husband paid what he owed. I could be totally way off base and this whole thing could be a huge mistake. There wasn't a lot of time to think everything through. I just went with my gut and decided I had to get you out of there, too."

"That's why you were going to the police?"

"Right. I wanted to tell them about the woman before Rafferty had time to feed her body to the gators. At this point, I'm sure he's hidden all the evidence, but at least I can get you to Mañuel Solera, my friend on the Puerto

Jiménez police force, and he can help you get safely back to San José and then catch a ride to the States."

He hesitated. "I can't guarantee your husband's safety, though. I'm sorry. He's still there on Suerte del Mar. The only thing we can do is contact him when we get to town and urge him to get the hell away from Rafferty while he still can. If it's any consolation, I don't think Rafferty will kill him. Dead men don't pay their debts."

She couldn't seem to work her brain around this. It seemed impossible, completely out of the realm of believability. James Rafferty as a cold-blooded enforcer? She couldn't quite reconcile that picture with the man she'd read about in such glowing terms.

To believe Galvez, she would have to buy both that premise and the idea that Bradley owed him some vast sum of money.

She thought back over her fiancé's behavior the last few months of their courtship and the four-month engagement that followed, culminating in his concentrated efforts to convince her to go through with the marriage despite his infidelity.

As he tried to change her mind about canceling the wedding, he had shown an edge of desperation very unlike the polished, confident Bradley Swidell.

Part of her had wanted to believe him, to go back to the way things had been when she finally had a course for her future, as the wife of her father's successor.

But she couldn't seem to shake the image of his assistant on her knees in front of him and she had finally— far too late—realized she could never marry a man she didn't love and no longer even respected.

Bradley hadn't taken her continued refusal well. She had attributed his reaction more to concerns about his position at Lambert Pharmaceuticals. But if Ren's hypothesis was true, perhaps Bradley was more worried about James Rafferty's reaction when he found out Bradley was no longer set to marry the Lambert heiress, thereby cementing his future fortune.

Could she believe Lorenzo Galvez? She looked at him, those chiseled features shadowed and mysterious.

She wasn't exactly the world's best judge of character—she'd been willing to marry Bradley Swidell, for heaven's sake—but some instinct prompted her to trust this man.

If what he said was true—and with every passing second, she became increasingly convinced of it—he had risked a great deal to extract her from Rafferty's estate.

He had risked *everything*.

If not for her, he would probably have been able to paddle his own kayak away from Suerte del Mar, leaving no trace of his identity for Rafferty to find. He would have been safe to report what he'd seen, instead of running for his life through the jungle.

Instead, he had played the gallant hero, risking his life for a complete stranger.

She didn't know what to say or think. The only thing she was clear on was that she'd had an extraordinarily lucky escape, for the second time in a few weeks.

Bradley had put her in this precarious position, she realized. He held a hundred percent of the responsibility for this predicament she found herself in.

Their whole courtship seemed like a calculated ploy now. She was willing to bet he had looked around for some solution to his mounting gambling debts and finally noticed his boss's pudgy, inept daughter. Wallace's only child, heiress to his vast fortune.

Whether Wallace had suggested the courtship himself or Bradley had come up with it on his own didn't matter. She had been stupid enough to fall for it and had even tried to convince herself she loved the man, while he had been after her money the whole time.

She let out a breath, fury suddenly roaring through her—at her own gullibility, at her father for doing his best to promote the match, and especially at Bradley, for putting her in this position without any thought to her as a person.

"That son of a bitch. That sleazy, money-grubbing rat bastard." She spewed every epithet she could think of, and a few particularly creative curses she made up as she went along.

Ren's eyes widened at her litany but he didn't interrupt until she started to wind down.

"Rafferty is all that and more," he finally said.

"Not Rafferty. Bradley Swidell."

"Who's Bradley Swidell?"

"The son of a bitch I was almost stupid enough to marry."

Chapter 5

Almost married.

Ren stared at her, trying to make sense of her words. *Almost* married was a far cry from hearts-and-flowers, meet-me-at-the-chapel wedded bliss. He shifted his gaze to her ring finger and felt ridiculous for not noticing the obvious absence of something slightly important like a wedding ring.

He felt just as ridiculous at the instant heat flaring through him. So she didn't have a husband. That didn't make her suddenly available, he reminded himself. Still, he couldn't contain his vast relief.

He wasn't a man who poached on another man's territory. His parents' example had showed him marriage vows were sacred. Anybody who messed with another man's wife deserved whatever fire-and-brimstone punishment was in store for him.

Hell, just fantasizing about a married woman made him feel wrong somehow. Since he'd done nothing but lust after Olivia Lambert since he grabbed her off the trail back at Suerte del Mar, he couldn't help being relieved he hadn't committed some grievous moral offense.

Olivia continued to curse with vivid creativity, making a number of violent threats that seemed completely jarring coming from a woman who appeared so soft and sweet.

"Whoa. Slow down," he finally said. "You told me you were on your honeymoon."

Her diatribe wound down and he watched color climb those high cheekbones. She nibbled the corner of her bottom lip, focusing her attention on the darkness beyond their shelter instead of him.

"Technically, I was," she answered slowly. "I am. Oh, this is *so* humiliating."

She let out a ragged breath. "The truth is, I called off the wedding two weeks ago after I walked in on Bradley and his personal assistant in a compromising position that's, um, technically still illegal in major sections of the South."

Her Texas drawl was far more pronounced than it had been earlier and she was blushing a fiery red, he could see in the pale lantern light. Sympathy for her washed away his lingering relief, and he wondered if her heart had been terribly broken by her fiancé's infidelity.

"But you came to Costa Rica by yourself anyway?"

She glared at him. "Do you have some kind of problem with the etiquette of that, Mr. I've-Got-A-Machete-And-I'm-Not-Afraid-To-Use-It?"

He smiled at her tartness, then was astonished that

he could find anything amusing in this whole miserable ordeal. "Not at all."

"The plane tickets were nonrefundable. First-class. It seemed stupid to let them both go to waste, especially when I genuinely needed a vacation after sending out six hundred notices that the wedding was off. I was already getting really tired of hearing the questions and the arguments and the snide little comments. So yes, I'm on my honeymoon by myself."

She lifted her chin, her Texas accent thick and sugary sweet. "And I have to say, it's just shaping up to be everything I ever dreamed. I've been kidnapped and shot at and almost bitten by a venomous snake. I've climbed a hundred feet up in the air and eaten beef pot roast from a plastic bag. I just can't imagine how it could get better."

He had to smile at her vinegar. At least she was fighting him instead of turning back into that panic-stricken waif she'd been in the early hours of their journey together.

Sicko that he apparently was, part of him was severely tempted to try his best to give her a honeymoon she would never forget.

He pushed away his attraction and focused on the more immediate questions sparked by her stunning disclosure.

"I'm assuming Rafferty knew you were here by yourself."

"I don't know. I told you, I haven't even met the man. But I'm assuming his people must have told him I arrived groomless after they picked me up in Puerto Jiménez by myself."

All this was conjecture, Ren knew, but if Rafferty was expecting a man who owed him money, he would *not* have been happy to find Olivia arriving by herself.

His temper would no doubt have made him unpredictable and even more dangerous.

"Did this, uh, Bradley know you were coming to Costa Rica without him?"

"I didn't tell him. Or anyone, really, except a couple of girlfriends I swore to secrecy. They tried to talk me out of it, by the way. I should have listened to them."

She smiled a little and Ren was captivated by the way the small change in expression dramatically lightened her features. "I wish I had my cell phone. Jen and Lucy would never believe I'm up in a tree house in the middle of the jungle with a machete-wielding turtle scientist."

She seemed a little more relaxed, he was pleased to hear. Getting some nourishment into her system had probably helped.

"Your cell phone is still in your beach bag, which I stuffed in my pack, but there's no service out here, I'm afraid. The only cell towers on the peninsula are in the vicinity surrounding Jiménez. You can call your friends and tell them all about it when you're on your way home."

"I'll certainly have an interesting story to tell at cocktail parties, won't I?"

As he watched her soft, lovely features lift into a tired smile, he was grateful all over again at whatever impulse had led him down that particular trail at just the moment she was coming from the other direction.

He hated the idea that except for that small quirk of fate, she might have been in Rafferty's hands at exactly this moment.

"You said you were supposed to meet Rafferty for dinner tonight?" he asked.

"One of his staff delivered an invitation when she

brought lunch." She shivered again, despite the still oppressive heat, and wrapped her arms around herself. "Are you absolutely certain about what you saw and heard? He really shot a woman in the head?"

"That's the only part of this whole thing I am certain about, Olivia. The woman was tied to a lawn chair. Rafferty stood over her for a moment, taunting the man with her, then shot her. That's all I can really tell you. As to his intentions toward you, I can't say. For all I know, he could have a dozen blondes stashed away on Suerte del Mar and could have been talking about any one of them."

She clutched her arms more tightly around herself. "No. It makes sense. Everything makes so much sense. I wanted a honeymoon in Tuscany. Somewhere quiet and serene and *civilized*. I'm sorry, but I'm not a nature girl. I like good food and Egyptian cotton sheets and…and air-conditioning."

"Not exactly on the tourist brochures for Costa Rica."

"Bradley insisted we come here. He wouldn't even consider any other destination, no matter how I pressed."

Nothing she said was making him feel any more fondly toward her erstwhile fiancé. The man sounded like a major prick and she was probably well rid of him, though he wouldn't be tactless enough to say so.

For all he knew, she might be heartbroken over the end of her engagement, though by the curses and imprecations she'd been hurling around a few moments ago, he had a hunch her feelings weren't a hundred percent engaged at this point.

"I couldn't figure out why he wanted so much to come here. He's not into hiking, he's not what you'd call an environmentalist, looking for the whole adventure-in-the-rain-forest thing. A quiet nature retreat didn't seem at all like his thing, but he was adamant. I should have known something was up. I was just so stupid."

She pressed a hand to her stomach as if she was going to be sick any moment, and he hurriedly passed her another of his dwindling supply of water bottles.

"You need to get some rest," he said as she sipped gingerly. "We've got a lot of ground to cover tomorrow if we want to make it to Port J before the afternoon rains hit."

"You must think I'm the world's biggest wimp."

"I think I've dragged you through a tremendous ordeal the last few hours," he answered quietly. "I'd be surprised if you weren't wrung out. You'll feel better after you sleep, I promise. Give me a minute and I'll hang a hammock for you."

She looked doubtful but didn't say anything as he pulled his rolled camp hammock out of his pack and tied it securely around the roof supports. The rain had slowed further, he noted.

The night was still alive with sound. He found a familiar comfort in the teeming sounds of life, but hoped she would be able to sleep through it. The nocturnal rain forest was not a quiet place.

"Here you go," he said when the hammock was ready.

"I can't sleep in that. No way. I'll just sleep here on the floor."

"It's surprisingly comfortable," he answered. "Come on, give it a try. I'll help you get in."

She hesitated, but finally straightened to her feet and inched toward him, keeping one hand braced on the trunk of the massive tree. He held the hammock as steady as possible for her as first she sat down, then she swung her legs up.

He stepped away and she gasped a little as the hammock swayed. "It's okay. You're not going anywhere, I promise."

She nodded a little and took in a deep, cleansing breath. After a moment, she relaxed further. "You're right. It is comfortable. If I can only forget I'm a thousand feet up in the air, I might even be able to close my eyes for five seconds."

He smiled. "Good night, Olivia. Things will seem better in the morning, I promise."

"Where are you sleeping?"

He pointed toward the floor of the tree house. "Any horizontal space will work for me."

He extinguished the lantern, checked the mosquito netting one last time, then stretched out not far from her. The wood slats of the tree house were cool and comfortable. Not quite like his bed back at the research station, but it would do.

He passed a pleasant few moments listening to her settle into the hammock amid the music of tree frogs and cicadas and nightjars. She finally must have found a comfortable position.

When several moments went by without a sound, he was certain she was asleep. He rolled to his side and had just closed his eyes, when her low, polite drawl took him by surprise.

"Mr. Galvez …"

He rolled over again with a small laugh. "It's Dr. Galvez, actually. But after everything we've been through tonight, I think you could safely call me Ren."

"Ren, then. If what you say is true, that Rafferty planned to use me as some kind of…of bargaining chip against Bradley, I…thank you for what you did tonight. You would have been able to escape much easier without the extra baggage of a complete stranger but you didn't."

He imagined her there on the hammock, her big blue eyes troubled and those lovely features twisted into a solemn expression.

"You risked your life to take me out of there," she went on, her voice little more than a low, sleepy purr. "I just wanted you to know I'm…grateful."

"I'm glad you're safe," he said gruffly, astonished by the warmth soaking through him at her words. "Get some sleep, Olivia."

He heard nothing more from that direction and had a feeling she was asleep before her name even crossed his lips.

Though he was physically exhausted from the adrenaline crash after paddling for an hour and then hiking hard for another two, on top of a full day of research, his mind churned, going over and over the events of the evening.

She was right. This would have all been much easier without her. On his own, he could have pushed through all the way to Port J and been sharing an Imperial with Manny at their favorite cantina.

Hell, if he'd been on his own, he could have paddled away in his own kayak and used his satellite phone to call Manny when he was far enough away to be out of earshot of anyone on Suerte del Mar.

He still wasn't sure what impulse had prompted him

to take her along, but he couldn't regret it. Things were tougher this way, but at least she was safer up here than she would have been at Rafferty's place.

The rain started up hard again. As he listened to it sizzle and splat on the leaves of the tree and the roof of their shelter, he gazed again at her gently swaying hammock.

None of this was his normal *modus operandi*. He was a researcher. A scientist. His world was data and graphs and counting egg hatches, not dodging bullets and killing snakes.

In many ways, he felt as if he'd been living in a bubble the last few years, focusing on nothing but his work. Like one of his turtles, he had been content lurking inside his shell.

He went into Port J a few times a month to pick up supplies and have a beer or two, and once in a while he had dinner with friends, usually other scientists or some of the American expatriates who made the peninsula their home.

But he preferred being on his own, just focusing on his work. Life was easier that way. Mercedes's death had taught him that.

From the moment he bumped into Olivia in that skimpy bikini, he had been yanked out of his comfortable self-involvement and into a terrifying world where he had another human being depending on him for her very survival.

The paradigm shift didn't sit well with him. He wasn't anybody's savior. God knows, he hadn't been able to save that woman back on Suerte del Mar. He had stood there behind a lipstick tree and watched James Rafferty blow her brains out without making any move to stop him.

And Mercedes.

He sure as hell hadn't been able to help Mercedes.

He didn't like to think about the terrible events of two years ago and the guilt he had lived with every day since then. It was far easier on his psyche to focus on his work, to shut out anything with the potential to make his soul bleed again.

In a few short hours, Olivia Lambert had somehow managed to pierce the hard defenses he had grown around his emotions. Already he cared about her and was scared to death he wouldn't be able to keep her safe.

Not this time, he vowed. He wasn't some frigging Indiana Jones out to save the world, but she was his responsibility. He would do everything within his power to make sure she arrived in one piece to Puerto Jiménez and caught a flight back to Texas, where she would be out of reach of James Rafferty and his goons.

He had no other choice.

Olivia awoke slowly, not sure at first where she was or why every muscle in her body ached as if she'd been kickboxing all night long. She shifted to find a more comfortable spot and her bed swayed alarmingly.

Maybe she had a hangover. Maybe that's why it sounded like a dozen imaginary wild monkeys were chattering in her ears. She blinked her eyes open and discovered an alien, completely unexpected world bathed in color and light and sound.

She was in a hammock, she realized. That's why her bed moved when she did. She was in a hammock in a tree house in the middle of the Costa Rican rain forest.

Merciful heaven.

Suddenly everything came rushing back as fragmented memories jostled through her mind—running down the beach at Suerte del Mar with her hands bound, that terrifying kayak ride across the waves, holding on for dear life as a darkly gorgeous scientist drove a Jeep through slick mud while shots rained down on them.

She decided it might be easier to close her eyes and pretend it was all some kind of bad dream.

It seemed like some Hollywood creation, a wild, unbelievable thriller—the kind of show she secretly adored.

Living it was something else entirely.

She couldn't believe it was real but she was, without question, in a hammock in the middle of the jungle wearing someone else's clothes. She couldn't argue with the facts.

Things like this didn't happen to Olivia Anne Lambert. In a few short weeks, she had gone from looking ahead to a safe, secure, *boring* future as Mrs. Bradley Swidell to breaking her engagement, escaping a ruthless killer and running headlong into the jungle with a sexy turtle researcher.

Well, her friends were always pushing her to expand her horizons and shake herself out of her rut. This might be a little more dramatic than they intended, but she'd come too far to turn back now.

What would Wallace have to say about all this, once she was safe back in Fort Worth? Nothing supportive, she could bet.

No doubt he would look at her with that painfully familiar disappointment in his eyes and tell her she was as impulsive and headstrong as her mother. If she had only followed through with the wedding, Wallace would probably opine, none of this would have happened.

She had to wonder if her father would sing the same refrain when she told him Ren's hypothesis—that Bradley was to blame for this whole thing, that he owed James Rafferty money in gambling debts and planned to use her trust fund to pay them off.

She still didn't know for sure if that was indeed the case, but she could easily believe it. Bradley loved money and the process of making it. He was heavily invested in the stock market and dabbled in day trading. She could imagine he would thrive on the challenge and risk of betting large sums of money against a man like James Rafferty.

She rolled over and slid out of the hammock. It was easy to understand how Bradley could be mixed up with Rafferty. It wasn't quite so easy to fathom how she could have let herself be caught up with *Bradley*.

She'd been a sucker. There was no other word for it. Bradley had waged a fierce campaign to woo and win her, and she had surrendered without much of a fight at all.

She burned with shame when she remembered how flattered she had been when he first turned all that charm and assiduous attention in her direction. He was an extraordinarily good-looking man and he had been powerful and successful, with the added bonus that he was her father's right-hand man.

For the first time in her life, she had experienced the warm glow of her father's approval and she had found it heady and addicting.

At the time, it had seemed wonderfully romantic. He claimed to be madly, passionately in love with her, and she had believed him. Now it all seemed so cold and calculated. He had probably already been in over his head with Rafferty six months ago when he had first started dating her.

She must have seemed a perfect pigeon, just ripe for plucking. His extraordinarily wealthy boss's quiet, plump, eager-to-please daughter who didn't have any kind of a social life to speak of because she was so terrified of turning into her mother.

Put so starkly, it filled her with shame but she couldn't deny the truth. For her entire life, Wallace had been holding up Maelene as an example of everything Olivia should fight against in her own psyche. Her mother had been self-indulgent, weak of character and loose of morals. How the two of them ever hooked up long enough to create her, she would never understand, but apparently Wallace at one time in his life had been drawn to those qualities in a woman, even a stripper like Maelene.

Her conception had been unintentional, she knew, the result of a wild affair, but Wallace had married the woman he impregnated, despite his own misgivings.

She didn't remember her mother at all—Maelene had died of a prescription drug overdose before Olivia was two years old—but her maternal grandmother had pictures in her little house. Her mother had been vividly pretty, in a blowsy kind of way, with the kind of smile that drew people to her.

She imagined living with a stern workaholic like Wallace couldn't have been an easy life for a woman with Maelene's vitality and *joie de vivre*.

The chatter of monkeys drew her mind away from her father, and she realized her dreams weren't being populated by imaginary creatures. A group of some eight or nine small white-faced monkeys were perched in an adjacent tree watching her.

With an incredible feat of gymnastics, the bravest of the lot swung from the tree onto the railing of her shelter and hopped back and forth along the narrow railing with amazing agility.

He was so close she could clearly see the quizzical expression on his face as he watched her.

"Hey there," she murmured, charmed by him.

The monkey made that chittering sound again as he hopped back and forth. An instant later, he disappeared below the tree house and her heart stuttered for a moment with fear that he might have fallen, until she reminded herself he was an acrobatic monkey.

Curiosity to see the view beyond their tree house warred with her natural fear of heights, but she finally summoned the nerve to edge to the railing of the tree house.

Awe quickly took the place of her fear at the sight unrolling before her eyes.

Everywhere she looked was color and light. She could see the ocean from here far below them, a vast and stunning blue. Closer to her were a hundred shades of green, emerald to mossy to pale, almost white.

The green was broken up by spots of vivid red, purple, orange and yellow from flowers growing profusely, even here in the canopy. There were moving spots of color, as well—huge, kaleidoscopic butterflies flitted through the trees, joined by birds with bright, extraordinary plumage.

Though the sun was just beginning to crest the hill behind her, the air was already muggy and close. But she didn't mind, entranced by the splendor spread out like a visual feast in front of her.

"Nice view, isn't it?"

She jerked around to discover Ren pulling himself back into the tree house.

This was her first chance to see him in full sun, and she had to keep from staring. He was gorgeous in the light—lean and dark and masculine. Even with his smile and the warm light in his brown eyes, he looked rugged and dangerous, maybe because of the dark stubble shadowing his face.

She cleared her throat. "I...yes. The, uh, view is wonderful."

His smile widened. "I love the ocean, but there's something to be said for the rain forest in the early morning light."

She managed a nod, her stomach trembling as he continued to look at her with that strange light in his eyes.

"You've been down and back up already?" she asked, then cursed the inanity of the question as soon as it left her mouth.

"I brought breakfast. You hungry?"

"Starving," she admitted, realizing with shock it was true.

He dropped a small hip pack and dumped a smorgasbord onto the tree house floor—green bananas, pineapple, mangoes, star fruit and a coconut. "I hope you like fruit."

Her mouth watered and she imagined the splendid tropical fruit compote she could make with this bounty of ingredients.

"They look delicious," she exclaimed.

He pulled out his machete and started slicing into the

pineapple. "I'm afraid I don't have plates, but those leaves work well in a pinch."

She braved the railing again and reached up to pluck several of the huge oval leaves. Ren, in turn, divided the fruit between them. For a few moments, they feasted in silence, surrounded by the noises of the jungle. It was a surreal experience, eating fresh fruit in a tree house in the rain forest while monkeys watched and brilliant tropical birds flitted through the trees.

"Did you sleep well?" he asked.

She nodded. "Better than I expected. I thought I would have nightmares the moment I closed my eyes. What about you? The floor couldn't have been comfortable."

"It wasn't bad. No bugs, no snakes. I've had worse nights."

He probably thrived on this sort of thing, the whole wilderness adventure thing. She had a feeling she and Ren Galvez were as different as salsa and ketchup.

"Where are we going?" she asked after a moment. "Can we see it from here?"

He pointed in the opposite direction from the ocean, east into the sun. "We need to head over the hills and then down again until we get to Rio El Tigre. There's a village there where we can catch the *colectivo* to Puerto Jiménez. You can just make out the trail through the canopy."

He leaned in to show her, until they were inches apart—so close she could smell the scent of his skin, soapy and male. Her nerves shivered and she had to fight to keep from leaning closer and inhaling.

Ren shifted his gaze from the jungle to her, and raw, wild awareness suddenly blossomed between them. Her breathing hitched, her stomach trembled and their vibrant surroundings seemed to fade as her attention focused wholly on him.

Just when she was certain he would kiss her, he blinked several times in rapid succession, let out a deep breath, then stepped away.

"We should, uh, probably head out before it gets much hotter."

"Right. Of course," she murmured. Much hotter than this and she would implode.

"There's water in the catch basin on the other side of the platform if you need to wash up. I put your beach bag over there and I set out a comb and some soap."

That must be why he smelled clean and fresh. She, on the other hand, was probably much less appealing.

It had been twenty-four hours since she last showered, and she'd hiked through the mud and muck for hours before going to sleep. Her hair was a tangled mess, she had no makeup on and she had a feeling she smelled decidedly ripe.

No wonder he hadn't wanted to kiss her!

She hadn't given a thought to her appearance since he grabbed her off the trail the evening before, but now she couldn't think of anything else. She could feel her face burn and turned away so he wouldn't see. "That would be good. Thanks."

She hurried to the basin he'd rigged on the other side of the platform and splashed her face with the warm water.

Wishing fiercely for a hot shower and the huge bag of toiletries she'd packed along, she yanked the comb through her hair while she chided herself for letting her hormones get stirred up over nothing. A man like him would never be interested in someone like her, and she would do well to remember that.

She scanned the contents of her beach bag, wishing she had something a little more useful in there than a romance novel, sunscreen and a cell phone without reception.

Still, she felt marginally better after using a corner of her beach towel to scrub her face and all the exposed skin she could reach—and even some of the unexposed, when she turned her back to him and stuck the towel furtively under her shirt. She did the best she could without a mirror to yank her hair back into a ponytail.

At last, there was nothing left to do but put on those dreaded boots again. She sat on the floor of the platform, eyeing them balefully.

Ren, busy returning things to his pack, caught her disgruntled expression. "I left out the first aid kit and set out some moleskin for your blisters. Let me take a look before you put on the shoes again."

She wasn't sure she could endure having him touch her sensitive feet again, not after the heat still twirling through her, but she didn't see what other choice she had.

He knelt before her and picked up her foot, peeling away the bandage with slow care. She tried to control a shiver as he gently applied more ointment, another bandage and then the moleskin.

By the time he finished her other foot, her nerves felt stretched to the breaking point.

"I'm sorry about the blisters. That should be a little better."

"I guess that's the price I pay for hiking through the jungle in boots that are too small. Still, they're better than my flip-flops."

He returned the first aid kid to his bulging pack. "Well, I'm sorry I didn't have a bigger size."

Despite the sizzle of awareness, she felt comfortable enough with him this morning to finally ask the question she'd been wondering about.

"Why do you have women's boots in the first place? Who do they belong to?"

His expression instantly changed as his mouth tightened and his eyes shuttered. "A former research partner."

She definitely sensed more to the story than just those few terse words. "They look like they've never been worn. Did she forget them when she moved on?"

He said nothing for a moment. Finally he spoke, his voice low and more solemn than she'd heard it. "She never had the chance to wear them before she died."

Oh Lord. Leave it to her to stick both feet—wearing a dead woman's boots—in her mouth.

"I'm so sorry, Ren."

He looked as if he was going to say more, then he closed his mouth abruptly and stood up.

"We need to get moving."

Chapter 6

His prisoner wasn't much of a whiner. He had to admire her for that.

After nearly two hours of hard hiking—mostly uphill in the burgeoning heat of the morning—her face was flushed, perspiration was dripping down her creamy skin and her hair was already coming out of the ponytail she had twisted it into.

She winced with every step and he knew her blisters had to be killing her right about now, but she still didn't complain once or even ask him to slow down.

He admired her strength of spirit even as he wondered how the hell he was going to push her for another five miles.

Though he set a steady pace for them, he was still moving much more slowly than he would have on his own. If not for her, he would have been in El Tigre by now, looking for a ride to Puerto Jiménez.

No, he corrected, he would have hiked all night and been in Port J hours ago.

But that scenario was all irrelevant. He was here on the trail five miles outside El Tigre, doing his best to keep her going when she looked hot, tired and discouraged.

"We can stop here for a few minutes," he said a few moments later. It was a natural stopping place, near a small waterfall on a spring-fed stream that eventually fed into Rio El Tigre.

With a bone-weary sigh, she sank to the ground, heedless of the mud that was ever present during the rainy season.

It was a nice spot to take a rest, with bright-colored birds flitting across the burbling water and orchids and heliconia growing in wild abundance amid the rich flora.

The air was thick with their perfume, and the sun filtered through the high leaves of the canopy, sending beams dancing on the ground in changing patterns. It might even have been romantic, if not for the urgency of their situation.

He handed her the last water bottle, which she took with alacrity. She gulped about half of it down in three swallows, then stopped and lowered the bottle from her mouth.

He stared at the water droplets clinging to those full, lush movie-star lips and couldn't seem to look away.

"Aren't you thirsty?" she asked.

Oh yeah.

"I'm okay," he lied, ignoring the sudden ache in his gut that he knew nothing else but tasting her would quench.

"Is this all the water we've got?"

He managed a smile. "Look around you. We're in a rain forest. I can find water."

"Surely not water that's safe to drink."

"Lucky for us, I've got a water filtration system in my pack and I've been keeping our empty water bottles, just waiting for a good spot to use the filter. It won't take long. Just rest while I take care of it."

He pulled the small filtration kit out of an outside pocket and set up the hosing, then started suctioning water out of the creek to pump it through the filter unit.

She watched the procedure with a fascinated interest he found both distracting and gratifying, in a weird sort of way.

"That just shows how stupid I am," she said after a moment. "I didn't even know such a thing was possible."

"You're not stupid."

"I certainly feel like it out here. I'm afraid I'm not very good at this."

He raised an eyebrow. "At what? Resting?"

She laughed, though it had a rough, exhausted note to it. "No. I can handle resting. Believe me, I'm re-markably good at that. It's the whole outdoors thing that leaves me feeling like…like a virgin in a whorehouse."

He gave a surprised bark of laughter. "Interesting metaphor, Miss Lambert."

"Sorry." He thought she was blushing, but he couldn't be sure whether it was from embarrassment or just the heat pressing in from every side. "It's something my grandmother would have said."

"I bet you're a lot like her."

A look of surprise flickered over her features. "I'm

not at all like her. She's brave and smart and out-spoken and…wonderful. I'm *nothing* like her."

"I don't know too many women who would have made it this far without ripping my head off."

"I've been tempted," she said wryly. "If I were a little taller, I might try."

"You've been great. I'm setting a tough pace and you're keeping up with me just fine."

"I'm just afraid you'll leave me behind for the white-lipped peccaries."

He laughed. "I wouldn't do that. We're in this together now. No turning back, Liv."

She stared at him for a long moment, an arrested look in her eyes, and he thought for a moment she wanted to smile back at him. But she hid her mouth in the curve of her shoulder, and he couldn't be sure.

He finished refilling the water bottles with filtered water. "Here we go. It's not quite Evian, but it will do for the rest of the trip. We've got about two hours before the rains hit."

She watched him package up the filtration system and return it to his backpack. "How do you know so much about survival in the jungle?"

He shrugged. "I've just picked it up here and there in the five or six years I've been in Costa Rica. It's not much different than hiking anywhere else. You just have to be aware of the heat and the dangers peculiar to an equatorial lowland rain forest."

"Where were you before you came here?"

He had a feeling she was only making conversation to extend their rest, but he didn't mind. It had been a long time since anybody had bothered to ask about his past.

"Here and there," he answered. "School, grad school. I went to college in Florida."

"You probably grew up traipsing around in the jungle."

He laughed. "Not quite. We don't have a lot of tropical rain forests in the Utah backcountry."

That clearly took her by surprise. Her blue eyes widened and she stared at him. "Utah. Really?"

"Tiny town called Moose Springs. You've probably never heard of it."

"No, I'm sorry. I went to Park City skiing with friends once a few years ago but that's all I know."

"Moose Springs isn't far from Park City. About thirty miles or so. One of my brothers is still there. He's the sheriff, if you can believe that. His wife's the town doctor."

"The sheriff? Really?"

"Just like in an old western. He wears a badge on his shirt and everything."

And he was fiercely in love with his wife, he didn't add. The last time Ren had been home to Moose Springs had been for Daniel's wedding to Lauren Maxwell. He almost hadn't gone, since it had only been three months after Mercedes died, when he was still lost in the grips of guilt and pain.

He would have been much happier here in Costa Rica, still stuck in a bottle and fighting with anybody who moved, but Anna, their little sister, had guilted him into it. She was very good at bossing the whole world around and especially enjoyed tormenting her brothers.

He remembered sitting in the little chapel in Moose Springs, hungover and jet-lagged. As he watched Daniel and Lauren and their radiant joy in each other, he had been quite sure his guts had somehow been ripped out and thrown there on the floor for everyone to see.

He let out a breath, pushing away the memory. Instead, he focused on Olivia Lambert as she sipped the rest of her water bottle and dabbed at the perspiration on her forehead with the sleeve of her T-shirt.

Leaves rustled high overhead, probably in a breeze they couldn't feel down here. Their slight movement sent a shaft of sunlight to encircle her and he couldn't seem to look away. She looked lovely here in the wildness of the rain forest, softer than the delicate orchids around them.

She met his gaze and for a moment, something flared between them, something bright and fragile. Then she looked away, leaving him curiously bereft.

"So tell me how a small town in Utah became the breeding ground for a turtle scientist who ended up in the wilds of Costa Rica," she asked after a moment.

He pushed away his odd reaction. "My dad had a brother who lived in central California. One summer when I was eight or nine, my parents packed us all up to visit my uncle and his family. While we were out there, we drove to the ocean and…I fell in love."

It seemed a mild understatement when he remembered standing on the seashore for the first time, a little kid from Utah who'd never seen a body of water bigger than the barren Great Salt Lake.

He had stood on the beach in Capitola staring out at the vastness of the ocean, the undulating waves and the sunlight glinting off the water and the white crests, and had been enchanted.

Captivated, entranced, completely bewitched.

During the same trip, he and his family had gone to the Monterey Aquarium and then whale-watching on Monterey Bay. By the time they returned to the wharf, he knew without a doubt he would spend his adult life studying the ocean and the creatures who lived there.

He had never regretted it, even during those worst days after Mercedes died.

"What about you?" he asked. "What do you do in real life, when you're not roughing it in the jungle on your solo honeymoon?"

She mumbled something but a jacana called at the same time.

"Sorry. I missed that."

"Nothing important," she answered, her voice stiff and the open curiosity gone from her eyes. "I work in human resources at my…at a large pharmaceutical company in Dallas. Or I did, anyway. I resigned right after I broke my engagement."

"Whoa," he exclaimed. "You don't do things half-way, do you?"

She made a face. "Obviously, you don't know me very well. My whole life has been about doing things halfway. Just ask my father."

If he had ever had a chance to talk to her father, he couldn't imagine the man would be very thrilled with him for putting his daughter in this kind of danger.

"I'll do that. I'll call him for a chat after I get us both safely to Puerto Jiménez and you on a plane bound for home."

She looked less than thrilled, though he wasn't quite sure whether it was at the prospect of him talking with her father or at the idea of catching a ride home.

"I'm sorry, but we should really get moving again."

She gazed at him for a long moment, then nodded slowly and stood, doing her best to hide a wince as she stood.

"I'm thinking we'll try a shortcut I've heard about a little ways ahead. It might cut off a couple miles of hiking for you. What do you think?"

"As long as we don't have to climb across a swamp full of alligators, a shortcut sounds wonderful."

Shortcut or not, the trail didn't get any easier.

Olivia plodded along, distracting herself from the burn in her thighs and the ache in her feet by focusing on the wild, exotic scenery around them.

She had always envisioned the rain forest as being lush and thick, nearly impossible to penetrate, much like the landscape at Suerte del Mar. The higher in elevation they climbed, though, it seemed the more open the understory became.

She wouldn't call it sparse, exactly, because low ferns, vines and bromeliads grew in wild abundance, but it wasn't like walking through the jungle in a Rudyard Kipling story, either. They had a fairly clear view ahead of them of fifty feet or more.

When she asked about it, Ren had explained that the canopy was so thick here that little light reached the forest floor.

Still, the rain forest teemed with life. Every inch of space seemed to be occupied by something living, from exquisite flowers to translucent blue morpho butterflies, to the monkeys screeching in the treetops.

And the trees and vines alone were incredibly beautiful. Some had twisted, crisscross shapes, others were spiraled and another had an accordion shape like a piece of hardtack Christmas candy.

Even though she was hot, tired and undeniably frightened, Olivia couldn't help being enthralled by the place, by the sheer wildness of this exotic place.

Take away the homicidal maniac chasing them, and she imagined plenty of people would pay big bucks for a guided tour like this. Ren was a walking font of information.

He had explained to her that the Gulfo Dulce Forest Reserve, where they were hiking, was a corridor to Corcovado National Park, the gem of Costa Rica's park system.

The Osa Peninsula was home to a staggering biodiversity, Ren told her—an estimated fifteen hundred plant species, eight hundred kinds of trees, nearly four hundred bird species and six thousand kinds of insects.

And that wasn't even counting the rich marine waters offshore, both on the Pacific and the Golfo Dulce—Sweet Gulf—on the other side.

She found herself fascinated by everything she passed, wanting to ask questions the entire way.

The whole thing seemed surreal. Forty-eight hours ago, she was in her climate-controlled condo in Fort Worth trying to decide which of her swimming suits showed the least amount of flab and picking through her to-be-read pile for paperbacks to take along.

She found it ironic now that she had boarded that plane at DFW feeling her life sucked and things really couldn't get much worse.

Her father wasn't speaking to her, she had no job, no

fiancé and had just spent two weeks returning early wedding presents and sending notice to the six hundred people who had been invited to the wedding.

The idea of leaving by herself on her honeymoon, of facing that empty seat beside her on the airplane, had been overwhelming, and she had thrown a major pity party for herself.

Now here she was, her feet pinched and probably bleeding again in too-small boots as she hiked through the hot tropics to God knew where with a machete-packing mad scientist—who just happened to be the most gorgeous creature she had ever encountered.

She felt wilted and completely out of shape and knew she had to be slowing him down dramatically, but Ren went out of his way to be encouraging and to laud her for keeping up with his pace.

She had a feeling she would never be Nature Girl, but there was a peculiar sense of accomplishment in this, in seeing this exotic part of the world most people would never have the chance to experience.

She wouldn't precisely say she was enjoying herself, but how could she help but appreciate the raw beauty they walked through?

Or the raw beauty of the man in front of her, who just now stopped on the trail with a frown.

"What's the matter?" she asked.

"I'm not sure we're going the right way."

"I thought you knew a shortcut."

"It's marked on my map, but the trail seems to be getting more and more narrow. Have you noticed that? I hope I haven't led us down a dead end."

He glanced at her, worry in his dark eyes. "Let's stop

here a minute. You can put your feet up and I'll head down the trail a little farther and see how things look. No sense you walking more than you have to."

Under other circumstances, she would have objected strenuously and argued that they should stick together. But she had suddenly discovered an urgent need to use *el baño,* so pressing she realized she must have been ignoring it for at least the last mile.

The thought of being alone out here in the jungle while Ren did a little reconnaissance work up the trail was only slightly less horrifying than having to announce her dilemma to him and having him accompany her into the bushes.

"Will you be okay?"

"Just come back."

He smiled. "I will, I promise. You need anything while I'm gone? Another water bottle or something?"

More liquid was the last thing she needed right now. "Um, no."

"Okay. I'll leave the pack here. Feel free to raid the pockets for whatever you need."

Please, God, let there be toilet tissue, she prayed. She managed to keep from digging into the pack until he walked out of sight. Then she furiously ripped through the outside pockets and breathed a huge sigh of relief when she found a roll of biodegradable tissue in the second place she looked.

Five minutes later, she returned to the trail feeling a million times better. Amazing what an empty bladder could do for her mood. She found a moss-covered log on the side of the trail, which ran along a small tributary. She was almost content as she listened to the sounds of the rain forest and tried to count the different species of birds and butterflies she could see in a ten-yard radius.

She had reached thirty when she suddenly heard a huge blast rip through the stillness.

She rose, her heart pounding. That sounded like a gunshot. What else could it possibly be?

Oh dear heavens. Had Rafferty found them? Her bones were frozen in an agony of indecision—she didn't know whether to climb the nearest tree, huddle here by the stream or run after Ren as fast as her aching legs would carry her.

Before she could reach a decision, two men suddenly materialized out of the jungle, stealthy as pumas.

She gasped, her brain quickly recording several salient details. Even without the shotguns, no way could she mistake this pair for a couple of nature lovers out for a pleasant hike through the jungle. These men were roughly dressed and filthy. They were young, she thought, possibly early twenties. One had a pitted, scarred face and cold dark eyes, and the other was huge, with a torn dirty shirt and a slightly vapid look on his features.

More important than their physical description, the smaller one carried a big, terrifying shotgun. They both stared at her as if *she* were the one who had just appeared out of nowhere, then they started yelling at her in rapid-fire Spanish.

She couldn't understand most of their words, but their body language clearly expressed outrage at her presence here on the trail, for reasons she couldn't begin to figure out.

Scarface brandished his shotgun at her suddenly as

they advanced on her, and her heart rate picked up another notch. Through it was a glimmer of anger. What was it with men in this blasted country, always shoving some kind of weapon in her face? She was getting darn tired of it.

He growled something harsh and guttural at her. When she didn't answer, he repeated the same words, his voice even harder.

"I'm sorry," she said, hating the tremble in her voice. "I don't understand. *No comprendo.*"

He raised the shotgun as if he was going to hit her with it, and she cowered against the trunk of a huge tree.

Were they Rafferty's men? Would the suave and smooth gambling mogul actually employ two men who looked so unkempt and who smelled as if they hadn't bathed in months?

Where was Ren? Her gaze shifted down the trail and she wished desperately for him to return.

"Who are you?" the scarred man asked in heavily accented English. "Why do you come here?"

"I wish I knew," she muttered.

He brandished the shotgun again, apparently unhappy with her flip answer and she tried to draw air into her lungs.

"I…my friend. *Amigo.* He brought me here."

"¿Donde esta?"

Where is he? At least that's what she thought they asked. Somewhere safe, she hoped, but since she couldn't say that, she simply shrugged.

"You lie. You are spy."

A spy? *Her?* She was the most unlikely spy in the universe. She would have laughed if she wasn't so terrified. She managed to shake her head. "No spy," she answered.

The smaller one stepped back, and she thought for a moment they would leave her alone. Then he said something quickly to the other one, the large, dense-looking one.

He grabbed her shirt suddenly with hands as huge as the leaves of the palmetto trees around and shoved her against the tree.

She nearly gagged at his rank, almost feral, body odor as the rough bark scraped her through the cotton of her shirt.

He pulled out a knife and held it to her throat, and she whimpered. She could only be grateful again for her now-empty bladder. "Please don't hurt me," she begged. "Whatever I did, I'm sorry."

"Uno mas," the other one said, his voice deadly hard. "What do you do here?"

She was weak-kneed with fear, afraid she would pass out at any moment now. Before she could summon an answer, a new voice intruded on the tableau.

"She's with me."

Ren! She nearly sobbed with relief and looked over the massive shoulder of the brute holding her, to find Ren standing behind Scarface with his machete across the man's neck.

He looked big and rough and dangerous, as if he would yank the machete across his throat without the slightest provocation, and she had never seen anything more wonderful in her entire life.

He spoke rapidly in Spanish to the men in a voice she had never heard from him before, one hard and fierce. The smaller man responded and for several moments they volleyed words back and forth. She could only pick up a few words here and there—*tortugas,* turtles, was one.

She wished to heaven she could understand more, but she clearly picked up the tension between them as they stood frozen—Ren with his machete at the smaller man's throat and his partner with a blade at hers.

How could they possibly win? He was one man against two, one armed with a shotgun and the other with a knife as sharp as that machete.

But to her surprise, a moment later Scarface dropped his shotgun to the dirt and gave a sharp command to the other man. The cold tip of the blade lifted from her neck, and the man stepped away so abruptly she stumbled to her knees.

As abruptly as this little drama began, it ended. Ren dropped his machete to his side though he didn't sheathe it again. The man whose neck it had recently adorned started to laugh and the other one did, as well.

Scarface came to her and reached a hand to help her to her feet. *"Lo siento, señora,"* he mumbled, then he and the other man slipped away back the way they had come.

She stared after them, wondering why she suddenly felt so woozy and odd. The heat pressed in on her, and the blood seemed to rush from her head.

"Are you okay?" Ren made it to her side in two steps. "Did they hurt you?"

"No," she mumbled, then the world started to fade and turned to black.

Chapter 7

He'd say this for her—Olivia Lambert certainly knew how to faint with grace.

One moment, she stood on the trail looking with baffled relief as her second set of kidnappers in twelve hours were swallowed by the rain forest; then she blinked once, twice, then crumpled as if someone had yanked the stuffing out of her.

He swiftly wrapped his arms around her, catching her before she could hit the ground. Fighting back his own relief that the men had left—and the lingering effects of the gut-clenching fear he had felt when he found her backed against a tree with a knife at her throat—he took her weight in his and lowered her with care.

"Olivia? Come on back, Liv."

Her sable lashes fluttered against the smooth, creamy skin of her cheeks but she didn't open her eyes.

Her skin was pale and covered with a fine film of perspiration and she had a smudge of dirt across her cheek. Despite it, she looked ethereal in his arms, like some kind of lush, sensual fertility goddess.

As he gave her a quick visual check to make sure the rough men hadn't hurt her, the tenderness welling up inside him scared the hell out of him.

"Olivia? Come on, sweetheart. Talk to me here."

She still didn't respond and his arms tightened. "I'm sorry but we don't have time for this. We've got to move before the rains hit. Come on, baby." He finally gave in to temptation and traced a thumb down her soft cheek, wiping away the dirt.

At his touch, her lashes fluttered again, looking impossibly dark against her skin. This time, her eyes opened. She gazed at him like a bemused little bird for several seconds, her eyes cloudy and baffled.

He again felt that weird tug in his chest when she lifted a corner of her mouth in a half smile. It slid quickly away and he watched as awareness returned to her eyes.

She scrambled to sit and he eased his hold, though some small part of him he was afraid to acknowledge was reluctant to let go.

"Those men! Where are they?"

"It's okay. They're gone. You're okay now. I've got you."

He wouldn't have expected her to find comfort from such a statement, but she relaxed a little against him and seemed content for now to stay there. "Who were they? They aren't from Suerte del Mar, are they?"

"Those two? No way. They're gold miners. Squatters who set up operations illegally in national parks and national forests. The Osa is lousy with them, though there aren't as many as there used to be. A few years ago the rural police worked with the federal government to clear them all out, but over the years some have returned."

"Why were they so angry at me?"

"My fault there." Guilt pinched at him and an echo of the fear that had gripped him when he saw her in danger.

"The shortcut I heard about would apparently lead us right through their operation," he explained. "Another half mile and we would be in the middle of it. Folks up here don't take kindly to strangers wandering where they're not wanted, and they must have been afraid you were spying on them or were after their windfall."

She was silent for a moment but made no move to leave his arms—much to his relief, since he didn't want to let go. She felt incredibly right in his arms, warm and soft and female.

"What will we do now?" she asked.

"Backtrack a mile or so and pick up the other trail. It's the only thing we can do at this point. I gave them my word."

"More hiking." She sounded completely dispirited at the idea and he tightened his arms.

"I'm sorry, Liv. I should have just stuck to the original trail in the first place. I just want to get you to safety as quickly as possible."

So far he was scoring a big fat zero in the protection department. He had dragged her away from Rafferty and thrust her right into more danger.

"What did you say to them to make them leave? I thought…I was sure they were going to kill us both. One moment, I thought we were dead and the next they disappeared. You must have been very persuasive."

He focused on the canopy above them. Gauging the clouds overhead and trying to ascertain the imminent risk of rain was far easier than trying to face her right now. "I, uh, told them who I was," he said after a moment.

"They know you?" she asked, surprise in her voice.

This revelation wasn't exactly going to inspire her with confidence that he could get her out of here safely, but he didn't see that he had any choice but to tell her the truth. "I guess they've heard of me. The population of the Osa Peninsula isn't that big. Maybe 6,000 people. And, uh, I have a bit of a reputation."

"A…reputation?"

He sighed. "A few of the locals call me the crazy turtle man."

He supposed he *had* gone a little crazy after Mercedes died, when he had ripped the Peninsula apart trying to unearth the men who burned down the station. Once they were found and turned over to the rural police to face charges, he thought he would feel better, that somehow accomplishing that deed would take away the terrible ache he couldn't breathe around.

He had been wrong. The craziness had still burned inside him. Desperate and guilty, he'd turned to the bottle then and he'd been a mean drunk, starting fights with anybody who looked at him crosswise.

He had been sober for eighteen months now—except for the occasional Imperial, he didn't drink much at all—but his reputation still followed him around like those dark clouds up there.

At least in this case, a little notoriety had come in handy.

He wasn't sure she would agree. After several more moments when she didn't say anything, he risked a look at her and found her watching him out of those huge blue eyes.

"You're probably thinking my, uh, unfortunate nickname explains a hell of a lot about the last twelve hours."

She shook her head. "I don't think you're crazy at all, Ren. I might have at first, but I've never been so glad to see anyone in all my life as I was that moment you came bursting through the trees."

He gazed back at her, stunned into speechlessness. Had anyone in his entire life ever looked at him with such total trust?

"Thank you," she went on. "That's twice now you've saved my life."

She lifted her face to his, her eyes soft and grateful. Her mouth was inches from his. He could cross that tiny space in a heartbeat, he knew. The temptation was overwhelming, all-consuming.

He could think of a million reasons why he shouldn't follow through on that urgent need. The miners could return at any moment, and he had given them his word he and Olivia would immediately turn around and head back the way they had come. The rains would be hitting soon, turning the whole trail into a slippery, sloggy hell. They had a long way to go before they reached Port J.

Yeah, all those things were important. But they paled against the overriding hunger gnawing in his gut to taste her.

He sighed and lowered his mouth the few inches to hers, abandoning every ounce of common sense.

Her mouth was warm and sweet, like biting into a fresh, ripe mango, and she sighed at the first touch of his lips.

He might have stopped after that brief, heady taste. But when she threw her arms around his neck and returned his kiss with unmistakable enthusiasm, he was lost. Heat surged through him, wild and potent and out of control, and he deepened the kiss.

She pressed herself against him, those miles of luscious curves that had haunted him since he saw her in the pale dusk on Suerte del Mar. He groaned, savoring the contrast between her softness and his instant hardness.

As her mouth tangled with his, he forgot every-thing—the squatters, Rafferty, the myriad dangers of the rain forest. All he could focus on was Olivia Lambert and the blood churning through his veins.

He wanted her. Right here, right now, with a hunger that roared through him like a jet fighter leaving con-trails through his psyche. He wanted to rip her clothes off and devour that soft skin, taste those curves.

Now *this* was paradise.

Olivia arched against him, her hands caressing his hair and those broad, powerful shoulders.

She had absolutely no experience with this wild hunger, this urgent, primal need to tangle her body with his right here on the jungle floor. His mouth—ah, his mouth!—was fierce and possessive and demanding. His matching hunger seemed to soothe all the battered nooks and crannies of her soul.

Until this moment in Ren's arms, she hadn't realized how humiliated she'd been by Bradley's infidelity, how she had been demoralized, her confidence in her own desirability completely shredded. Finding out Bradley had wanted to marry her for her money had finished the job his personal assistant's Lewinsky had started.

None of that seemed important right now. It was all as distant as her dingy little office at Lambert Pharmaceuticals. For now, this vital, gorgeous man wanted *her*—dumpy, out-of-shape Olivia Lambert—and she found the passion in his kiss an incredible aphrodisiac.

She shivered as his strong hands tugged up her borrowed T-shirt and played at the bare skin above her waist. Her hands slid beneath his shirt to clutch at the hard muscles of his back.

His fingers drifted further north and she held her breath, waiting for him to reach the bikini top she still wore under her clothes. Just before he did, a huge explosion boomed through the jungle.

She froze, her breathing ragged, and drew her mouth away from his.

"What was that?" she murmured.

"Nothing. Shotgun blast." He trailed kisses along her jawline and she nearly forgot her train of thought. But *nothing* and *shotgun blast* were not phrases normally associated with each other in her mind and she couldn't quite get past that.

She drew in a shuddering breath and started the complicated process of extricating herself from the tangle of his body around hers. "Wh-who's shooting?"

It took Ren several seconds to answer, and she saw with some surprise that his eyes looked slightly unfocused and a pulse beat rapidly in his neck. "Uh, probably our buddies, the squatters, out looking for lunch, I'd guess."

She couldn't seem to breathe. All she could focus on was the grim realization that she had virtually attacked Ren Galvez in the dirt in the middle of the rain forest. Another sixty seconds and she would have had his shirt off and be exploring all those hard muscles and interesting angles.

Why, again, had she stopped?

She drew in another breath. She wasn't her mother. She had spent a lifetime trying to control the traces of Maelene that threatened to emerge at odd moments.

"What are they shooting at?"

He shrugged, still looking disoriented. "Could be anything. Iguana, Macaw. Whatever they find."

He gazed at her for a long moment, and she could feel herself flush at the heat still lingering in his brown eyes.

He must think she was some kind of desperate scorned bride willing to jump anybody warm who came along.

She wasn't. She *wasn't*. Making out with a man she barely knew was just not the kind of thing she did. She hadn't even kissed Bradley until their fourth or fifth date, and that had been nothing to write home about.

Not like the embrace she and Ren had just shared. That was worth a whole lot more than just a measly letter home.

She licked her lips, tasting him there still. What was happening to her? This wasn't her.

Sex was another area where she had pretty aptly demonstrated over the years she was a complete and abysmal failure. She supposed some women were just naturally good at it. She wasn't. She never knew what to put where, how to respond, where to touch.

She had learned early not to give in to any excess of

passion or she would earn a stern reprimand from her father. *Stop that. You're acting like your mother.* How many times had she heard the words from her father?

As a result, she acquainted everything her mother had been with something undesirable. From everything she'd pieced together, Maelene had been lush and sensual, a drama queen, given to impulse. As a result, Olivia had tried, with limited success, to eradicate all those elements of her own personality.

She knew she was stilted and uncomfortable in the bedroom. She certainly didn't catch fire in an instant simply from the intoxicating taste of a man's mouth on her.

She must have malaria or something. Dengue fever, maybe. That was the only possible explanation for this insanity.

She rose to her feet. "We should, um, head out, don't you think? Since we're going to have to backtrack and all."

She found some small solace that Ren still looked as if he'd been smacked on the head by a falling coconut.

"Right. You're right." He took a breath and shook his head slightly as if to clear it, then gave her a careful look. "You okay?"

She knew perfectly well he wasn't referring to the encounter with the squatters. She tried to offer a cool smile, despite the blush that crawled over her features. "Why wouldn't I be? I know we were simply reacting to the stress of the moment. It didn't mean anything."

"Right. Of course it didn't."

Conversely, his quick agreement annoyed the heck out of her, but she decided not to let it bother her.

"What were you saying about rushing to beat the afternoon rains? Let's go, then."

He gazed at her for a long moment, his dark eyes intense, searching. Then he nodded and rose as well, shouldering his pack on the way up. "You're absolutely right."

The next two hours were a blur of misery. He pushed them both hard, so hard she had to fight back tears at the ache in her muscles. Her poor feet would never be the same, she was very much afraid.

She tried to ignore her discomfort, focusing instead on the exotic splendor of the rain forest, though it was a tough sell to her aching muscles. Ren no longer seemed inclined to point out a colorful bird here or a unique plant there. In fact, he was brusque, bordering on uncommunicative, and she discovered without his expert commentary, everything sort of lumped together into a big wall of green.

Still, she tried to pick out the few plants and wildlife she recognized to pass the time. What she tried *not* to do was dwell on that stunning kiss and the hormones still zinging crazily through her body.

Darn him anyway for getting her so stirred up, setting fire to this deep yearning inside her for more.

Finally they reached the summit of the highest mountain and started down the other side. She could see the blue of the Golfo Dulce spread out before them, with the mainland on the other side.

Not long now, she thought, trying not to sob with relief. Surely she could make it a little longer.

And then it started to rain.

Like the rains of the night before, there was no warning drizzle or even a stray droplet or two. One moment the trail was dry, the next they were trapped in the deluge that instantly soaked them both and turned the trail into a slick mess.

He didn't stop even then, the monster, and she decided she definitely hated him.

Those few moments of stunning heat were an aberration. She couldn't possibly be so fiercely attracted to such an inhuman machine.

The trail channeled all the runoff from the trees above them and they were soon slogging through ankle-thick mud that stuck to her boot with every step. In no time, she was coated in it up to her knees.

Still Ren pressed on down the hill without even looking back to see if she followed. She plowed along behind him, cursing him the whole way, then suddenly stumbled on some impediment on the trail, a rock or a tree root, maybe, concealed by the mud.

Arms flailing, she struggled to keep her balance on the slippery trail but it was a losing battle. Her boots slid out from under her, and gravity did the rest.

She could only be grateful Ren's back was to her so he missed her ignominious, completely graceless slide into the mud. She managed to keep her face clear of the muck, but that was the only portion of her anatomy that escaped.

The fall snatched the breath from her chest and for several seconds she could do nothing but lay there in the cold, sticky mud trying to catch it again, aching and trembling and miserable.

How much lower could she sink? she wondered. She thought she'd hit bottom two weeks ago when she called off her wedding. But then, being kidnapped on her solitary honeymoon showed her she could slide a little lower. And now this seemed the absolute bottom. There couldn't possibly be anywhere left to go but up from here.

Her father was right. She was a complete and utter failure. A walking disaster. She drew in a shaky breath, then another and another, aware of hysteria hovering in the wings.

Her life was a joke. *She* was a joke.

She let other people tell her what to do—her father, Bradley, even Ren. Other women might have put up a fuss when a stranger jumped out of the jungle with a machete.

Not Olivia.

She had gone with him without a murmur. Okay, she might have showed a little belated spirit by trying to escape and run away down the beach near his research station, but she hadn't had any kind of concrete plan, had just acted from delayed instinct.

After he caught her, she had just gone along with whatever he wanted of her. Climb a tree? Sure. Sleep in a swaying hammock a hundred feet in the air? No problem. Hike behind him for miles, until she could barely move? Sign me up.

She was tired of it. She sat in the middle of the rain forest covered in mud from head to toe and more disheartened than she'd ever been in her life. She couldn't do this anymore. Not the hike, though that was miserable enough, but the way she'd been living her life for twenty-six years.

From this point on, she was done trying to please everyone else. She was going to grab hold of life on her own terms, damn it.

Ren must have finally realized she wasn't trudging along behind him like a good little soldier. He turned around and even from twenty feet away and even in the middle of a blinding rain storm, she could see surprise register on his dark, masculine features, then concern.

He hurried toward her. "Liv, what happened? Are you okay?"

"Swell," she muttered. "Can't you tell?"

As he moved closer, she stared at him in disbelief. No way. It couldn't be possible, but somehow Lorenzo Galvez had just slogged through a damn monsoon rain and come through with only his boots covered in mud.

He was soaked, his T-shirt molding to strong, chiseled muscle, but he was somehow still relatively clean.

Red-hot fury exploded in her. Even before she fell, she had been coated in the stuff up to her thighs, each step splattering more and more on her skin.

Now it was in her hair, covering her shirt, soaking through the cotton fabric to insinuate into every nook and cranny of her person, and the fact that he had emerged unscathed from this torment he was inflicting on her seemed the worst sort of injustice.

She wasn't anybody's wuss anymore. Hadn't she just decided that? She would never be a superhero, but she could damn well correct this particular wrong.

Without stopping to think it through, she dug her fists into the inches-deep mud and picked up a good, juicy handful. She drew in a deep breath, took aim and let it fly.

It was a lucky shot. The wad of mud plopped against his cheek with a satisfying thud.

With mud dripping off his cheek, he gazed at her as if she were nuts.

"Why the hell did you do that?"

"Sorry," she lied, then demonstrated her complete lack of repentance by picking up another glob and chucking it at him. This one splashed against the hard planes of his chest and dripped down below his rib cage. "There. A few more and we'll be a matched set."

He gazed at her for a long moment, then the edges of his mouth twitched. She almost didn't mind sitting there covered from head to toe in mud, not if it would earn her a breathtaking smile like the one that spread over his features.

"You are a piece of work, Olivia Lambert." Something that looked almost like affection sparked in those cinnamon eyes. "Right now, I have to say I'm very glad I didn't let Rafferty have you."

"You're just trying to sweet-talk me so I won't throw more mud."

He smiled. "That too."

It was ridiculous. Hadn't she just decided she was at the lowest point in her life? So why should she feel this warmth burst within her like a balloon filled with confetti?

"If I try to help you up, you're not going to do something completely unoriginal like yank me down into the mud with you, are you?"

She tilted her head, considering, as rain dripped from her eyelashes. "Tempting. Very tempting. But then we'd both be stuck down here."

He held a strong hand out to her. She gripped his fingers and he pulled her to her feet. He didn't release her immediately. She was intensely aware of him, the strength of his fingers holding hers, the warmth of his breath on her cheek, the scent of him, masculine and alluring.

She thought for a moment he would kiss her again

and she caught her breath, holding every twitching muscle immobile. Instead, he lifted the edge of his T-shirt, sacrificing a clean corner of it to wipe at the mud on her throat and jawline.

Her gaze met his and there was a strange, glittery expression there she couldn't begin to interpret. She drew a shaky breath as the intimate tenderness of the gesture sent the last of her defenses tumbling.

When he was done, he stepped quickly away. "We're not making any progress here. We might as well stop and grab a bite to eat until the rains ease a little."

She wanted to press a hand to her trembling stomach, but she was afraid to reveal the effect he had on her. Instead, she stood in the rain watching him pull a small folded tarp and some rope out of his miracle pack. In moments, he had rigged a tented shelter for them between a couple of trees.

By the time he finished, the torrents of rain had sluiced the worst of the mud from her clothes and skin.

All she needed now was a little shampoo and some French-milled soap and she might feel halfway human again.

There was barely room for the two of them under the tarp but she climbed in and sat down. Though the improvised shelter did a good job of keeping most of the rain out, it wasn't dry, by any stretch of the imagination. Still, it was better than the alternative.

He sat beside her, pulling the survival pack behind him, and the tiny shelter immediately shrunk.

"I've never seen rain like this," she said. "When the tourist brochures say this is the rainy season, they're not kidding."

"September and October are the wettest months on the peninsula."

"Does it really rain twice a day?"

"This time of year, yeah. We don't see much rain from December to March but the rainy season makes up for it."

"A heck of a time for a honeymoon, I guess."

Something dark and sultry sparked in his eyes, and her stomach muscles clenched. She had a vivid image of wrapping herself around him in a warm, clean bed somewhere while rain pounded the windows outside.

A muscle in his jaw twitched but he quickly looked away, digging through the contents of his pack. A moment later, he pulled out a couple granola bars and a packet of beef jerky.

Quite a departure from the lunch she had enjoyed the day before at Rafferty's estate—perfectly poached sea bass with a delectable pineapple-mango salsa—but she suddenly discovered she was hungry enough to eat the tarp covering them.

"Sorry I can't offer you something better." Ren opened the wrapper of the granola bar and handed it over to her. "I cook a mean chicken fajita and caramel flan."

Her mouth watered just imagining it, but she forced herself to chew and swallow the stale granola bar that tasted as if it had been at the bottom of his pack for some time. "So not only can you rig a shelter in the middle of a rainstorm in two minutes flat but you cook, too. A man of many talents."

He grinned. "I'm glad you think so."

Some wolfish light in his eyes reminded her of their kiss, the intimacy they had shared and the awareness burning through her at such close quarters.

"How did you learn to cook?" she asked to distract herself from the knowledge of how easy it would be to span the short distance between them and taste that hard mouth again.

"My mom taught me and my two brothers and sister some traditional Mexican dishes when I was a kid, but I never enjoyed it much. I would have much preferred being outside in the grass on my stomach watching the ants scurry around."

"If you love bugs, I imagine Costa Rica must be a regular paradise for you."

He gestured to the pounding rain outside their tiny shelter. "What's not to love?"

She couldn't help but smile. He gazed at her for a moment, then shifted his gaze to his own granola bar.

"I've been glad of my mama's lessons in the kitchen over the years. I would have starved to death without them. They would have found me hunched over my data, my withered, emaciated frame clutching my last granola bar."

She didn't even like imagining such a fate. "Don't you get lonely working by yourself all the time?"

"I'm not alone all the time. I have volunteers who help me count egg hatches sometimes, and I've shared space on and off with other researchers."

"That's right," she suddenly remembered. "You said you had a research partner. The woman whose, um, boots I'm wearing." The woman who had died, she remembered.

Ren was silent and any trace of lightheartedness seemed to seep away, leaving his features hard and unyielding.

"Mercedes Mora," he said after a long moment. "She was affiliated with *La Universidad de Costa Rica*. We were working on a joint project studying the effects of organochlorine contaminants on olive riddley sea turtle immunity."

She had no idea what *organochlorine* meant or even what an olive riddley sea turtle looked like. But she knew with surety there had been more between Ren and his partner than a research project.

She should let the subject drop, she thought, but she was suddenly deeply curious about the woman whose shoes she was literally filling. A woman he must have cared about.

"You said she died. What happened to her?" she finally asked.

He gazed out at the now drizzling rain, but not before she saw a haunted pain flicker in his dark eyes.

He didn't answer for several moments. When he did, his voice was taut and sharp-edged. "Our research station caught fire while I was out in the field collecting data one day. Probably arson. The fire investigator flown in from San Juan speculated that Mercedes was napping when the fire started and died from smoke inhalation without even waking up."

Olivia shivered, both from the hideous fate of his partner and from the dispassionate tone he tried—and failed—to use. She could hear echoes of pain in his low voice though he tried to hide it and her heart ached for his loss.

"Did they have suspects?" she asked quietly.

"Plenty of them, unfortunately. A lot of Ticos on the coasts aren't all that crazy about the work I do. Sea turtle eggs have been a traditional local delicacy. We try to work out a deal where they can harvest eggs the first forty-eight hours after they're laid, but we sometimes get a less-than-cooperative reception when we try to block access to nesting sites."

He sighed. "The day before the fire, Mercedes and I had a confrontation with some poachers from the village. It was pretty nasty, but I never imagined they would go that far. I think they only wanted to stop our research and get us the hell out of there so they could go back to the way they'd been doing things for generations. I don't think murder was their intention, but that's the way it turned out."

She thought her life was so terrible, with a cheating fiancé and a perpetually disappointed father. Her problems seemed so petty compared to the loss he had suffered.

"I'm so sorry, Ren." She touched his arm, and his muscles were tight beneath her fingers. "She was more to you than just a research partner, wasn't she?"

She thought at first he would answer her, and he took a deep breath as if gearing up to agree. She waited breathlessly, but he only gazed out into the rain forest beyond their shelter.

"The rain's letting up," he finally said. "I guess our lunch break is over."

Without another word, he climbed out and started taking down the tarp.

Chapter 8

At the pace he was setting, most women he knew would have dug their heels into the mud and told him to go suck a pineapple. Though he could feel the waves of fatigue radiating off her, Olivia didn't complain. Other than that momentary breakdown on the trail earlier, she gave no sign that the going was tough on her.

He had never met anyone like her. She was a mass of contradictions—vulnerable one moment, tough as steel the next. He had a feeling a man could spend his whole life with her and not discover all her secrets.

Not him, of course. He wasn't a forever kind of guy. His life was his work and that's all he had room to deal with.

He glanced at their surroundings, recognizing the curve of the tributary they followed. Another twenty minutes or so and they should hit El Tigre.

Assuming they could make it in time to catch the regular "bus"—really just a beat-up four-wheel-drive pickup truck with bench seats in the bed covered by a tarp—they should be in Puerto Jiménez an hour after that.

She could be on a plane to the capital by dark.

It would be a vast relief to know she was safe. She could contact the embassy in San José for help getting out of the country. He didn't know her family situation—she'd mentioned a father, he was almost certain—but he would make sure she had someone at home to look out for her.

The thought of saying goodbye sent a weird little pain twisting through his chest. It was crazy. He barely knew the woman. But somehow he knew the events of this day would leave an indelible imprint on him.

He paused to check her progress as they descended a moderately steep slope. She wasn't watching the trail, her attention fixed on a small troop of squirrel monkeys climbing a nearby tree, which gave him an opportunity to watch *her*.

She had a little mud on her cheek and her hair looked bedraggled in its makeshift ponytail, but there was still a radiance to her that glowed through everything.

She was so fragile and lovely, a soft American Beauty rose amid the exotic foliage of the jungle, and she took his breath away.

Her fiancé must have been the stupidest son of a bitch who ever lived. Why would a guy who had *this*—all those lush curves, that orchid-soft skin, the tantalizing mystery of her—risk it all by messing around with another woman?

It made absolutely no sense to him. The guy ought to be strung up by his *cojones* for hurting her.

A fierce protectiveness swelled inside him. She had been through enough. He had to get her safely through the rest of it.

"What's wrong?" she asked as she reached him. "Why are we stopping?"

"You need to drink something."

She made a face but pulled out the water bottle and obediently swallowed a few swigs of its filtered contents.

"Happy now?" she asked.

He wouldn't be happy until she was safely off the peninsula.

No, he corrected himself grimly. Her departure certainly wouldn't make him happy, since she would take all that radiance with her. He would miss her when she was back in her safe little life in Texas.

"We're almost to El Tigre," he said instead of answering. "No doubt Rafferty has stationed some of his goons there. We'll have to come up with a disguise for both of us."

"I think I've already demonstrated I make a fairly terrifying mudbog monster."

He smiled. "I'm afraid we'll have to come up with something a little more believable."

Forty-five minutes later, he stood back and surveyed his handiwork.

"I look a mess, don't I?" she asked, self-doubt in her voice as she surveyed her attire.

"Not at all. Just…different."

It was a pretty good disguise, if he did say so himself, for something improvised on the spur of the moment.

They had caught what felt like their first damn break

since he stepped foot on Suerte del Mar when they encountered a woman doing laundry near the river on the outskirts of the village.

Ren had paid the astonished *campesina* an exorbitant amount for a rough-hewn blouse and skirt for Olivia and a pair of men's work trousers and shirt for him.

The woman—Maria Ramos—had been reluctant to part with the clothes at first, but with what he paid her, she could buy decent replacement clothes and feed her family for at least a month.

Her husband's work attire was a decent fit for him, though the pants were on the short side. But Maria hadn't been a small woman, by any stretch of the imagination, and her clothes swamped Olivia, even with her generous curves.

After a moment of thought, Ren had come up with a solution.

Olivia patted her abdomen now, distended a good eight inches by the padding he'd improvised using the blanket in his bedroll.

"Never in a million years will I pass as a pregnant woman."

"Sure you will. People see what they want to see. If you act like you're expecting a blessed event any moment now, that's what people will see. Let's try the hat."

He set the big floppy hat he'd purchased from Maria Ramos on her head and tried to tuck as much of her hair under it as possible.

He tried three or four times, trying not to notice the softness of her hair under his rough hands, but it was no use. No matter what he tried, telltale blond tendrils slipped free.

"It's not working, is it?" she asked.

"No. And that's a problem. Rafferty's men will be looking for me and a blond woman. We're going to have to figure something else out."

"Like what?"

He looked around, his mind spinning with possibilities. He finally found what he was looking for off the trail a dozen feet or so.

"Be right back," he told her, then cut a path through the thick undergrowth with his machete until he reached the tree he was looking for.

Genipa Americana.

He returned to the trail and quickly found a stone with a slight indentation. It would probably do the trick.

"Hand me that rock over there," he said.

She pried it out of the mud and brought it to him, then stood watching as he crushed berries from the bush between the two rocks and mixed water with them, making a thick paste.

"Do I dare ask what you're doing?"

He glanced up. "You're not going to like it," he predicted.

"I have a sneaking suspicion you're right."

When the paste was ready, he beckoned her to sit on a fallen log.

"I'm sorry about this but we'll never get through town with you as a blond woman, even with the hat. It's just too risky."

Dawning horror spread over her features. "No way. You're not putting that stuff in my hair!"

"We don't have a choice, Liv. It will be fine, I promise."

"What is it?"

"Indigenous tribes here and in the Amazon use genipa leaves to dye their hair and skin for rituals. I'm not worried about your skin since Ticos have a wide variety of skin tones. But your hair's a dead giveaway and we just can't take that risk. You'll never pass as a native unless we hide it and this is the only way except for cutting it off."

"Tell me this isn't permanent," she begged. "It will wash out, right?"

"I'm sure it will." It was stretching the truth a bit, since he wasn't sure of any such thing, but he decided he'd better not tell her that.

She shuddered and for a moment she looked as if she were going to cry, but she finally sat obediently on a log.

"Do you have any idea what you're doing?"

"Not really," he admitted. "I just thought I'd put the paste in and that would do the trick."

She sighed. "You're crazy. And I'm even more crazy to let you do this."

Still, she didn't protest when he applied the paste to her hair and eyebrows, hiding any trace of blond he could find. Between the two of them, they decided to let it sit for ten minutes and then tested a strand. It wasn't as dark as his, but she was no longer so obviously blond.

"Close enough," he said. "Lean over my arm and I'll rinse the rest of it off."

She obeyed, resting her neck on his left forearm. He was again awash in tenderness that she trusted him enough to do all this. He wanted to hold her close, to kiss the vulnerable soft skin of her neck bared by her position, but he forced himself to concentrate on the job at hand. Finally the last of the genipa was rinsed from her hair.

While Ren threw on the rough cotton clothes he'd bought from Maria Ramos, she ran his comb through her hair then quickly braided it to further disguise the color and topped it off with the big floppy hat.

"Well? Will I do?"

He studied her. Up close, no one would possibly mistake her for anything other than what she was— an extraordinarily lovely woman masquerading as a frumpy pregnant villager.

He would just have to hope to hell none of Rafferty's men managed to get that close.

"You'll do," he said gruffly. On impulse, he grabbed her close for a quick embrace, a hard lump of worry in his stomach at what they faced on this last leg of their journey.

She wrapped her arms around his waist and held on as if he were the only solid thing in her world. Despite her generous curves, she felt slight and fragile in his arms, and he wanted to keep her right here forever where she was safe.

He cared about this woman and he couldn't bear the idea of something happening to her. The tenderness soaking through him scared the hell out of him. He didn't want it, but he had no idea how to go back to the way things had been before she stumbled into his life.

He had the odd thought as he held her that he was like one of his turtles, that he had been hiding under his carapace since Mercedes died, unwilling to creep out and see if the world had gone on without him.

But somehow Olivia Lambert had lifted up his shell, exposing the man he used to be underneath.

"We should go," he murmured.

She drew in a deep breath and stepped away. "I'm ready."

He knew his high-dollar survival pack would look incongruent carried by someone dressed in rough farm worker clothes, so he'd condensed their most essential items into one of the cinch sacks from his pack.

Now he hefted the cinch sack over his shoulder and headed toward the main dirt road that followed the river the seven miles between El Tigre and Puerto Jiménez.

They might have been better off sticking to the rain forest and away from populated areas the rest of the way to Puerto Jiménez. If he were by himself, that's probably what he would have done: just hiked to town. But she was reaching her limit and he couldn't put her through more than necessary.

He just had to keep his fingers crossed that he'd made the right choice for both of them.

They skirted the dozen or so buildings of El Tigre and headed out of town. He kept a careful eye out for Rafferty's men.

To his vast relief, they caught their second break of the day after only a few moments of walking along the road when he heard the rumble of an engine. A moment later, the *colectivo* rattled into view, heading in the right direction.

His heart pounding as he considered all the possibilities of who else might be aboard, Ren kept Olivia out of sight in the bushes while he flagged it down.

The driver stopped, looking disgruntled at the delay. A quick glance in the back of the pickup told him it was full of the usual assortment of villagers and hikers coming out of Coronado National Park. Ren gestured to Olivia to come out of the bushes, then bickered with the driver, who didn't look thrilled at picking up two new passengers.

"My wife is having her baby soon and she goes to stay with her sister in Golfito near the hospital," he said. "You have to take us."

After a rousing argument, the driver finally relented and Ren handed her into the back of the truck. They squeezed onto the bench seats along the side and he pulled her close, trying to act the concerned husband.

The driver barely waited for them to sit down before grinding the truck into gear and rumbling down the road. She jolted against him and hung on tight, turning her face into his chest.

It was all he could do not to kiss her right then for having the common sense to conceal her features, just in case.

A nice bonus, Ren thought, having one last chance to hold her. He liked having her close to him, he admitted. He probably liked it far too much for their safety—and he definitely liked it too much for his peace of mind!

After everything they had been through so far, how was it possible she smelled so good?

The other occupants of the *colectivo* looked at him with interest.

"Every day she is sick," he said in Spanish.

The pair of hikers on her other side grimaced a little and slid away slightly, but the villagers didn't seem to mind.

"I do not know how she can grow so big with the baby when no food stays down," he went on.

"You will have a good strong boy, then." A large,

matronly woman in a pink dress and rubber boots smiled at them.

"God willing," he answered, giving Olivia a squeeze.

For the next forty minutes, they bumped along with the other passengers as the *colectivo* rumbled along the dirt road toward the gulf and Puerto Jiménez. The truck was stuck in mud several times along the journey and at one point it slid precariously close to the river's edge as the driver tried to extricate the tires.

Olivia gasped and Ren pulled her closer. "It's okay," he whispered in her ear and she immediately relaxed. Again, he was humbled and overwhelmed by her complete trust in him.

For most of the ride, they didn't pass another vehicle on the road. When traffic increased, he knew they were reaching Puerto Jiménez.

A sense of relief washed through him. Almost there, though he knew they weren't out of the woods yet. That was reinforced as they reached the outskirts of town and the public transit vehicle suddenly slowed.

They were approaching a queue of other vehicles and Ren's unease blossomed. He craned to see what was causing the delay and then hissed an oath in her ear.

"What is it?" she whispered.

"Roadblock up ahead," he murmured tightly.

She stiffened and began to tremble. His mind raced trying to come up with some way to get them both off the *colectivo*.

"What's going on?" he asked the woman across from them in Spanish.

She shrugged. "I heard on the radio some crazy man

kidnapped a rich American woman outside Carate. They are looking everywhere for her."

One of the young hikers—from Australia, judging by their accents—translated the woman's words to his companion.

"She said it's probably about the missing woman we heard about on the radio in El Tigre," he said in English.

"Didn't they say she was some kind of heiress?" the other hiker asked.

"Right. Worth millions. I'd love to find her. Her old man's in the prescription drug business. He'd probably be willing to pay a pretty penny to get her back."

Ren didn't have time to absorb that stunning information or the new dimension it added to this whole damn mess. The pickup truck pulled closer, now about five vehicles from the checkpoint.

"We've got to get out of here," he whispered to her. "Can you come up with a distraction?"

Her floppy hat bumped his chin as she nodded against his chest. An instant later, she straightened and started making retching sounds.

The tourists from Down Under edged further away. Ren didn't have to pretend much to look panic-stricken. He jumped out of the truck and helped her out while the villagers looked on in concern.

Olivia stumbled to the bushes and pretended to throw up while Ren stood by trying to look like a concerned husband. "I cannot take much more of this," he said to no one in particular. "*Pobrecita*. I hope she has this baby soon."

The villagers looked on in sympathy.

"The bumping, it is making her sick," Ren said. "We

will walk to the port from here to catch the water taxi to Golfito. It's not far."

No one on the *colectivo* seemed to think anything of it. Ren slung an arm around her shoulders and walked across the road. It was easy enough when they were out of view of the vehicle, concealed by a large water truck, to slip through the first break in the trees they could find.

Ren had to use his machete for several yards but quickly found a trail through the thick growth. Finally when they were several hundred yards away from the roadblock, he let loose.

"A damn *heiress*. Why didn't you tell me?"

She bristled, though she didn't stop walking. "Excuse me, but I've been a little busy running for my life here."

He had no idea why he found the discovery so upsetting. All he could think about was how this complicated an already tangled situation.

"Let's define our terms here. How much of an heiress are we talking about?"

She looked reluctant to answer him but finally gave in. "Have you heard of Lambert Pharmaceuticals? My father is Wallace Lambert, the, um, founder of the company."

Lambert frigging Pharmaceuticals? He would have laughed if the whole thing wasn't so damn ridiculous. The company was one of the big boys. Her father had to be worth hundreds of millions, if not billions.

She had to be used to a life of luxury. Boarding schools, private yachts, silk sheets. And he had just dragged her miles through the jungle, feeding her MREs and granola bars and dying her hair with genipa that might or might not wash out, for hell's sake.

He felt like a fool. Worse, he felt betrayed that she

hadn't mentioned this little detail of her life to him. The distance between them had just become a huge, unbreachable chasm.

"Your father probably has the whole country looking for you by now. He's probably frantic with worry."

"I really doubt that," she muttered.

He sighed, trying to figure out what the hell to do with her now. Things were much easier when he thought only Rafferty and maybe the rural police in this area might be looking for them. With her father's resources, God knows who else might be on their trail.

He'd love to turn her over to her father or her father's minions and wash his hands of this whole mess. He would still have to deal with Rafferty, but at least Olivia would be out of it.

But he still didn't know who to trust. Until he figured that out, he figured they were best just to stick with their original plan to contact Manny Solera at the Jiménez police station.

They passed a house that looked familiar and Ren suddenly realized where their escape route had led them.

"I know this area," he said. "I've got a couple of friends with a beach bungalow not far from here. Bobbi and Al Fremont. Expats from Chicago. They've gone back to the States during the rainy season but I'm sure they won't mind us using their place for a few hours to clean up. Maybe you can crash for a bit while I call Mañuel Solera to see about arranging a flight out of here for you."

"You're just going to break in?"

The doubt in her voice—such a contrast to her complete trust of the last few hours—grated. "We're not going to steal anything, except maybe a change of clothes. If it bothers your conscience so much, you can always have Daddy pay them back."

She flashed him a quick look but said nothing, just followed as he took off down the trail.

She couldn't understand this man.

Okay, she had never been all that brilliant about figuring out the way *any* man's mind worked. They were all a baffling mystery to her. But Ren Galvez was in a class by himself when it came to murky, indecipherable male behavior.

He seemed a completely different man now than he'd been all day. For most of the day since leaving the tree house that morning, he had joked with her and teased her and pushed her along.

Now he barely looked at her, and he seemed to simmer with anger for reasons she couldn't begin to understand.

She hadn't done anything wrong. It wasn't *her* fault her father was Wallace Lambert. She would have vastly preferred a normal suburban father who pulled into the garage from work at five every afternoon and came to her dance recitals and helped her with her math homework.

"This is it," he said tersely when they reached a bungalow set back from the gravel road. There were no other houses in sight, as far as she could tell. The Gulfo Dulce couldn't be far off. Though she couldn't see it through the thick trees, she could smell the sea, a low, salty undertone to the sweeter, earthier scents of the rain forest.

"You're sure they won't mind?" she was compelled to ask.

"Positive. Just keep your fingers crossed that I can remember where they keep a spare key."

He finally found one under a loose board on the porch steps and unlocked the door, then held it open for her to proceed him.

The air inside the house had a close, steamy feel to it, but Ren quickly opened the windows and a breeze heavy with impending evening rain washed through.

It was a lovely home, with what looked to be native wood walls and floors covered in bright area rugs and comfortable furnishings.

She wouldn't have cared if it was a hovel. She was just so glad to finally be indoors, she wanted to stretch out on one of those area rugs and not move for a month.

"I'm going to call Manny. Why don't you take a shower and get cleaned up? I'm sure you can find something clean of Bobbi's in the bedroom to put on."

She almost burst into tears at the miraculous concept of indoor plumbing. "A shower would be nice," she murmured, which was possibly the most blatant understatement she had ever uttered.

He hadn't looked at her once since they entered the house. She didn't care, she told herself. Soon this would all be over and she would be on her way home.

The thought had no appeal whatsoever so she pushed it away for the more immediate pleasure of flush toilets and running water.

She quickly shrugged out of her clothes and for the first time caught sight of herself in the wood-framed mirror above the sink.

Oh. My. Word.

No wonder he didn't want to look at her. *She* didn't

want to look either! She looked atrocious, a bedraggled, pathetic stranger with sunburned skin and hair the color of old coconut husks.

Please, God, let this gunk wash out, she prayed as she stepped into the shower, then she forgot all about her hair in the sheer ecstasy of heated jets of water hitting her skin.

She washed her hair five times using apple-scented shampoo she found in the shower, until no more brown dye and leftover mud washed into the drain.

She used up all the warm water in the process, too bad for Ren. Let him think she was a spoiled heiress, she thought. He probably did anyway.

A half hour later, she felt almost human again. She brushed her damp hair and slipped into a pale yellow sleeveless dress she found hanging in the bedroom closet, then padded barefoot to the open living area.

She found Ren standing in the kitchen sipping what looked like imported American beer and gazing out the open window at the evening rain that had started up again.

He must have heard her approach because he lowered his bottle and turned. Then he simply stared at her, something wild and dark and alluring that she didn't recognize at first kindling to life in his eyes.

"The, uh, shower's all yours," she managed, in a voice that came out scratchy and rough.

Hunger, she realized. That was what she saw in the dark depths of his eyes.

Ren Galvez was looking at her like he wanted to devour her in one big bite.

Chapter 9

The silence stretched between them, so taut the air seemed to quiver with it.

Suddenly she was back in the rain forest with him, once more in his arms as his mouth explored hers with heartbreaking tenderness, his body hard and possessive against hers.

Her breathing quickened and heat flickered through her. She wanted to be there again, wanted it with a fierce ache, though she would willingly forgo the mud of the trail for nice clean carpet.

While the rain sizzled and crackled outside, their gazes held. She thought for a moment he would reach for her but instead he looked away, shifting his attention to the rain outside and the darkening sky.

"Uh, bad news," he said, his voice gruff. "Solera isn't available until morning. According to the desk sergeant, he's on a case. Yours, I would guess. All the rural police on the peninsula are probably working your kidnapping case, too bad for us."

She drew in a breath, ordering her unruly hormones to settle. With his glum tone, he couldn't have made it more clear that he was anxious to be rid of her, despite the heat between them.

"What do we do now?" she finally asked.

"Wait here until morning when he's back in the office, I guess. I don't know what else to do. Manny is the only one I know and trust on the police force. I would hate to talk to the wrong person and end up with you back in Rafferty's hands."

At least he wasn't so eager to be rid of her that he would turn her over to just anyone.

"I'm sorry," he went on. "I know you're anxious to be on your way, but I'm afraid you're stuck here for another day."

She wasn't sorry. She was in no hurry to return to Fort Worth and her father and the recriminations she knew she would face for placing herself in harm's way and putting others to all the bother and fuss of having to look for her.

She cringed just thinking about it, then caught herself. Okay, maybe she shouldn't have come on her honeymoon alone. She had been running away, escaping the social and emotional upheaval from breaking her engagement. It had been selfish and cowardly to leave.

But none of the rest of this was her fault.

Bradley Swidell was to blame, and she would be damned if she would let her father make her feel guilty.

"I don't mind," she finally answered Ren. "It will be lovely to sleep in a real bed tonight."

He cleared his throat, that glittery look in his eyes again. "Uh, right."

She had a vivid mental picture of sharing that bed with *him*, bodies entwined and mouths tangled under the mosquito netting. Hunger and need washed through her like that hard tropical rain outside, and she could feel heat soaking her cheeks.

"How was your shower?" he asked after a long, charged moment, then immediately looked as if he hadn't said anything.

"Heavenly," she answered. "I'm afraid I used up all the hot water washing my hair."

"Looks like most of the *genipa* came out."

"Most. Not quite all. A few more shampoos and I'm sure it will, though."

Were they really having a conversation about hair dye, she wondered, while what she really wanted to do was jump him right here in the kitchen?

"After I get cleaned up, I'll work on raiding the cupboards for something to eat."

"I'll see what I can find while you're showering."

"You don't have to do that. I don't know much about proper kidnapping etiquette here but I'm pretty sure it's my responsibility to feed you."

She shook her head. "You didn't kidnap me, Ren. You rescued me. I might be a spoiled rich heiress, but even I know the difference."

Something warm kindled in his eyes, and his mouth twisted into his first smile since finding out her father was Wallace Lambert.

She basked in that smile, in the slight lessening of the tension between them.

"Well, rescue or kidnapping, whatever it was, just sit tight while I shower and I'll find some dinner when I'm done. Maybe you could catch a nap or something. I'm sure you're exhausted."

By all rights, she should be, but energy zinged through her veins and she felt as if she could walk out that door and retrace their steps to the other coast without breaking a sweat.

He must have taken her silence for acquiescence. Big mistake. Olivia had no intention of sitting helplessly by.

She waited in the kitchen until he disappeared down the hall. Then she started opening cabinets to ponder her options.

For the last twenty-four hours, Ren had been the one in his element. He knew how to filter water, how to find food, how to hide their tracks. She had been as helpless as a toddler out there.

She would have perished in the jungle without him, would have been bitten by a snake or fallen off a cliff or something.

But in here, she wasn't helpless. She wasn't good at much in life, but no matter what her father said, cooking was one of her few talents.

Ren Galvez had saved her life. She had no doubt whatsoever. He had extricated her from Suerte del Mar at great personal risk to himself and then had helped her survive the rigors of the jungle to make it this far. He had showed her things about herself she never would have guessed, such as that she had the strength of will to overcome her terror and climb a tree when she didn't have any other choice.

She owed him a huge debt, one she could never repay. She could at least take this small burden from his shoulders.

The small bathroom was still steamy from her shower and smelled of apples and warm, clean female.

He was so damned aroused he couldn't think straight.

Ren closed the door behind him, trying to block from his mind the memory of how she had looked standing there with her hair damp and her cheeks flushed from the shower.

He was in serious trouble here. He had never wanted anything as much as he wanted Olivia Lambert.

If it were purely a physical response to her, he could handle this all much better. But he couldn't deny the emotional tug between them. He cared about her. If he didn't, he wouldn't have this tangled knot in his stomach, knowing there could never be anything between them.

They were worlds apart, just about as disparate as two people could ever be.

Money had never been at all important to him. He had grown up poor as dirt, though he hadn't fully realized it until he was in junior high and discovered kids he went to school with had more clothes than two or three shirts and one decent pair of jeans.

His parents had been happy if they could put food on the table. They were illegal immigrants who did whatever had to be done to feed their four children.

Though his family never had anything extra, he and his brothers and sister had always known they were loved. They had also always known their parents didn't judge people by how much money they had but how they lived their lives, trite as that sounded.

As a struggling college student and then grad student, Ren had learned to live on very little. He was happy with a small savings account and a healthy retirement portfolio and he had never wanted anything else. He drove an eight-year-old Jeep—if the jungle hadn't claimed it by now, anyway—and lived in a two-room concrete research station.

What the hell would he ever have to offer the daughter of the man who founded Lambert Pharmaceuticals?

Nothing. Not one damn thing.

He was a scientist consumed by his work. He was lousy at anything else.

He sighed as he whipped his shirt over his head. He knew it with his brain, but his body had plenty of things it wanted to offer her.

He couldn't help thinking it would have been better for both of them if Manny had been available. By now, she could have been on her way to the U.S. Embassy in San José instead of in the other room offering way too much temptation.

She was attracted to him.

He hadn't missed the signs there. He wasn't being egotistical when he acknowledged that he could probably walk back into that kitchen and seduce her in a heartbeat.

She was coming off a bad engagement and was probably vulnerable and needy.

If he were a different kind of man, he wouldn't hesitate to take advantage of that. He had been a long,

long time without a woman, and he had never known one who inflamed him like Olivia Lambert.

But he wasn't a different sort of man. He couldn't use her like that, just to slake a sudden hunger for soft, curvy blonds.

Better to just clamp down on his need and do his best to forget about how delicious she looked just out of the shower, though he had a feeling keeping those images out of his head was like trying to dam up Rio El Tigre with a handful of pebbles.

He turned on the shower spray and was almost relieved when, as she predicted, there seemed to be no hot water.

The water was cool, not cold—more refreshing than punishing. When he finished ten minutes later, he convinced himself he'd clamped down on most of his hunger for her.

He found a change of clothes of Al's and was returning his disposable razor to his toiletries bag in the cinch sack when he spied her beach bag at the bottom.

He pulled it out, intending to return it to her, then suddenly remembered her cell phone.

He could call her father.

The thought whispered through his mind and he pushed aside the mosquito netting to sit down on the bed as he considered.

Wallace Lambert would come for her, he didn't doubt it. She would be safe from Rafferty.

And safe from Ren.

He dug through her bag until he found her phone. He hit the button to turn it on, holding his breath to see if it had juice.

Not a full charge, he saw, but two bars showed up on

the power indicator. As he expected, it showed there was coverage here, since Al and Bobbi's bungalow wasn't far from the cell tower in Puerto Jiménez.

He stared at the phone, mulling what to do.

He didn't have another option. Not really.

Before he could reconsider, he scrolled through her address book until he found an entry labeled simply *Wallace*.

He hit the country code for the U.S. then dialed the number before he could change his mind.

Voice messaging picked up after the first ring, a terse, abrupt male voice—her father—and Ren drew in a deep breath.

"My name is Lorenzo Galvez. I'm a scientist on the Osa Peninsula of Costa Rica. Your daughter Olivia is with me. Whatever you've heard, I did not, I repeat, did not kidnap Olivia for any nefarious reason. She is completely unharmed and free to go at any time but she is still in danger. It would be best if you could come to get her. We're in a house outside Port Jiménez."

He quickly gave the address and directions to Al and Bobbi's house then hung up, hoping with every fiber of his soul that he hadn't just made a terrible mistake.

Olivia listened to the sounds of the shower coming from the bathroom and tried not to picture that strong, lithe body standing soapy and wet under the warm spray.

The kitchen was alive with other noises—the burble of water just coming to a boil on the stove for pasta, the rain cascading outside, the sizzle of sautéing onions.

So why couldn't she seem to focus on anything but that shower?

It took all her powers of concentration to force her attention back to the vegetables she was chopping.

The kitchen smelled even better than it sounded, the doughy scent of her no-rise breadsticks in the oven melding perfectly with the onions and garlic from her sauce.

She had definitely lucked out in the provisions department. The cupboards had been largely left bare except for stock supplies such as spices by owners who obviously expected to be gone for some time. But out the window she had spied an overgrown vegetable garden, lush with ripe, forgotten produce. Tomatoes, squash, yellow peppers, fresh basil. Everything she could possibly want for a lush harvest feast.

Someone here loved to cook. She could tell not only by the produce in the garden but by the quality of the knives and the cooking utensils. The kitchen was well laid out, with everything she might need within easy reach.

With only a few moments' work washing and peeling and slicing, she had all the ingredients for her favorite pasta primavera and cucumber salad.

She added fusilli to the boiling water and checked the breadsticks. Though the kitchen was warm, a moist breeze blew in through the windows and Olivia was in her element, so comfortable here that she even hummed a little in her terribly off-key voice.

"Madre de Dios."

At the muttered oath, she jerked around from the stove to find Ren standing in the doorway. His dark hair was wet and combed. He must have found a razor somewhere, she saw with some regret, since the sexy, disreputable stubble was gone.

He was wearing borrowed clothing again, a navy blue golf shirt and tan cargo shorts. He looked lean and dark and gorgeous.

She swallowed hard and had to fight all her instincts to keep from pressing a hand to the sudden nerves jumping in her stomach.

"What's all this?" He advanced into the kitchen area of the open floor plan. "I'm gone for twenty minutes and return to paradise. It smells divine in here."

She had to agree, except just now she couldn't smell any of the vegetables, only clean, delicious male.

"What can I do?"

A hundred possibilities flooded her brain, none of which she could share with him. "Um, you could set the table. It will all be ready in about ten minutes."

"Great. My stomach is already growling."

He seemed to know where everything was in the kitchen and quickly found plates and silverware and carried them to the dining area of the house. He pulled wineglasses from a cabinet and set them at the table, as well, then returned to the kitchen, leaning a hip against the breakfast bar while he watched her work.

She was never comfortable having an audience observe her messy cooking style and his close scrutiny made her flush. She was painfully aware of the subtle tension seething between them, of the jittery nerves jumping around her stomach and the itch under her skin.

She drained the fusilli and then tossed it with the sauce and vegetables, then sprinkled parmesan she'd found in the refrigerator over the whole thing.

When she pulled the breadsticks from the oven,

Ren stared. "How did you throw this all together so quickly?"

She shrugged, flattered by his look of astonishment.

"Luck, more than anything. I stumbled onto the vegetables and herbs in the garden, ripe and fresh as if they were just waiting for us. I made the breadsticks from an old no-rise recipe my grandmother used to make. I'm afraid dessert will be simple, just gingered fruit."

"Simple. Right." He shook his head, still looking astounded. "Let's see if Al and Bobbi have any wine to go with this delicious feast."

He found the perfect Chianti and poured her a glass, taking water for himself. The rain continued to spatter outside, but here it seemed as if they were wrapped in a cocoon of intimacy she found as seductive as it was wonderful.

He tucked into the food with gratifying eagerness. After the first bite, he closed his eyes with an appreciative moan.

"This is without question the best thing I've eaten in months. Maybe even years. When we were talking about our culinary skills back in the rain forest, you forgot to mention you were a genius in the kitchen."

She laughed, a blush heating her cheeks. "I'm not. Far from it."

He took another bite of the pasta, then followed it with a breadstick. "You should have a restaurant. I'm serious. You would be famous."

"That's the last thing I want. To be famous, I mean. But I did dream of opening a restaurant once."

"Why didn't you?"

She sighed and set down her fork, the lettuce suddenly tasting bitter in her mouth. She picked up her wineglass, though she knew even the Chianti wouldn't wash the taste of her failure away.

She had come so close to doing just that, opening a restaurant, right after she graduated from college. She had even come up with a business plan and hired an agency to scout locations. But she'd abandoned the idea after only a raised eyebrow and a few derogatory comments from her father.

Most restaurants fail in their first year. The Dallas-Fort Worth area had a glut of eateries. Did she really think she knew enough about business to make it a success?

Like water dripping on stone, he had worn away her confidence, as he always did, and she had lost the dream somewhere along the way. When he suggested she work at Lambert for a few years in human resources until she had a better understanding of the business world, she gave in.

Five years later, she was still there. Or at least, she had been until two weeks ago.

She didn't have to give up that dream. She swallowed the rest of her wine as the realization washed through her.

To hell with her father and his constant disapproval. She was now unemployed, with a world of possibilities spread out before her.

She had come of age to take control of her trust fund a year ago. It was long past time she took control of her life. There was no conceivable reason she couldn't open a restaurant if she wanted, or two or three or ten, for that matter.

When she returned to Texas, she would set the wheels in motion.

Or maybe when this was all over, she would just throw the last of her good sense to the wind and open a restaurant down here for tourists.

"If this brilliance is just your hobby, why are you stuck in human resources? Isn't that what you said you did?"

"Right. Until two weeks ago, I worked at Lambert Pharmaceuticals."

"Your father's company." He sounded annoyed again, for reasons she couldn't begin to understand. "I take it Swidell worked at the company, too."

"You could say that. He's the chief financial officer. My father's right-hand man."

She did her best to keep the bitterness from her voice, but she was afraid some filtered through anyway when he gave her a careful look.

"Daddy must have been royally annoyed at him for screwing around on his baby girl."

She let out a breath. "Not quite."

She should just stop here. Ren didn't need to know all the pathetic details. But somehow the words escaped before she could call them back.

"He took Bradley's side. My father couldn't understand why I would possibly want to break the engagement over such a little indiscretion. After all, we weren't even married yet. Why should I possibly be upset? A man is entitled to sow his last wild oats, right?"

"Not in my book," Ren said tersely, furious at her bastard of a fiancé all over again.

She blinked at his vehemence. "Well, my father didn't agree. He was furious with me for messing up something he had wanted since the day Bradley came to work for the company. He hasn't spoken with me since I broke the engagement."

Though she obviously tried to hide it, Ren heard the low, suppressed pain in her voice and realized her father had wounded her terribly. He ached for her, as well. What kind of father treated his child like an asset to be merged for his own gain?

His own father had been a constant source of strength to him during his life and had instilled honor and dignity in all of his children. Growing up, Ren had never doubted his father would back him in any fight he took on, as long as the cause was just.

He had always known his father was proud of him, that he and his siblings were his greatest joy.

Roberto Galvez had died in a construction accident while Ren was in grad school, and Ren still missed him every day.

With his life experience, he couldn't understand a man like Wallace Lambert. If he had a daughter and any man treated her in this humiliating and demoralizing way, Ren would rip the guy from limb to limb, not throw a childish tantrum aimed at the injured party.

No wonder she doubted her father would be trying to find her.

Damn, he suddenly remembered, the pasta suddenly tasteless in his mouth. He had called the man not thirty minutes ago.

Her cell phone sat like a millstone in his pocket. He had given Olivia's whereabouts up to a man who thought she should go ahead and marry a bastard who was already cheating on her before they even made it to the chapel, that she should consign herself to a life of adultery and broken vows.

"I'm so sorry, Olivia," he said.

She misinterpreted his apology as general words of sympathy. She shrugged. "I've been disappointing my father all my life. This was nothing new, just maybe a little more intense. You know, the craziest part is that I didn't even love Bradley. I only agreed to date him in the first place because it seemed to make my father so happy. And then I was caught up in everything until it all spiraled out of my control. For the first time in my life, I felt as if I had done something right, something that would finally make my father proud of me."

She winced and poured more wine—her third glass, he thought, but he didn't say anything.

"Pathetic, isn't it? A shrink would have a field day poking and prodding into my messed-up psyche. I mean, what kind of person would even consider marrying a man she didn't love, would spend the rest of her life miserable and unhappy, just to please her father?"

He had to tell her about the phone call. The knowledge sat heavy in his gut. "Olivia—" he began, but she cut him off.

"Don't you dare feel sorry for me, Ren Galvez."

He raised an eyebrow, distracted. "Is that what you think? I don't feel sorry for you. Not by a long shot. I think you had a lucky escape."

She laughed, though he thought it had a slightly tipsy edge to it. "You're absolutely right. I'm the luckiest woman in the whole wide world. I can't believe I even considered marrying him. I thought I was using my head, for once, when I agreed to marry Bradley."

She gestured with her wineglass. "You'd think I would figure out it could never work between us when I could barely stand to have him touch me. No, that's not true. I didn't dislike it, I was just…bored."

He suddenly hoped to hell she told Bradley Swidell exactly that when she broke off their engagement. It would serve the son of a bitch right.

"I thought it was me, that I was somehow incapable of…of any grand heat, any all-consuming passion. Bradley seemed convinced I must be frigid, though he was certain I would grow out of it once we were married. Or maybe he didn't care, as long as he had access to my father's money."

"You're not frigid." He could say that with unequivocal certainty, remembering her heated response to him back in the rain forest. "He was just an idiot."

She laughed again and he was entranced by her, even when she was a shade on the loopy side.

"I know. I figured that out when you kissed me today. I have to tell you, Dr. Lorenzo Galvez, I never knew it was possible to feel so…so alive, so on fire. I wanted to jump you right there in the jungle."

Chapter 10

He stared at her, lost to everything but his sudden fierce desire.

He was instantly aroused—and painfully aware that they were alone in the house with a heavy rain falling outside and a wide, comfortable bed only a few feet away.

He could have her there in a heartbeat, could assuage his hunger at last. It was the only chance he would ever have to taste that mouth, to be surrounded by her warmth and her soft curves. He wanted to take that chance more than he wanted his next breath.

"Olivia—" he began.

Whatever he meant to say was lost when she blinked and suddenly set down her wineglass, looking horrified.

"Oh no. Tell me I didn't just say out loud that I wanted to jump you."

"Yeah," he growled. "Yeah, you did."

Her color leached away, then returned in a hot, fiery tide. "Don't listen to me. It's the wine talking. It…it must be."

He drew in a shaky breath, feeling as if she'd just dumped the rest of the Chianti on his head. "Right. The wine."

It was exactly the reminder he needed. As much as he wanted her, he couldn't do a damn thing about it. Not under these circumstances.

She wasn't thinking clearly or she never would have made such a confession—and part of his personal credo was never to take advantage of any woman who wasn't completely, enthusiastically, one hundred percent in full command of her faculties.

"Forget I said anything," she muttered. "Forget I'm even here."

As if he ever could. He sighed. He should tell her now that he'd called her father. Before he could, she stood up and started clearing away their plates, her attention focused on anything but him.

He slid his chair back and rose. "I can do this. You went to all the trouble cooking. I'll clean up."

"I'm a messy cook," she protested.

"I don't mind," he assured her. "Those were the rules when I was a kid. If you don't cook it, you get to clean it up. Just sit down and rest."

She looked as if she wanted to argue but finally she shrugged, still avoiding his gaze, and moved to the living area. She sat down on one of the two armchairs angled to look out the wide windows overlooking the Gulfo Dulce.

Despite her protestations of her messy cooking style,

it only took him a few moments to wash and dry the dishes she'd used.

He quickly cleaned up the mess, vowing as he finished that he would tell her what he'd done.

If her father received the message, he would be here by morning to collect her. Judging by what she'd told him about her father, she would need a little time to prepare herself for Wallace Lambert's arrival.

But when he returned the last dish to the cabinet and joined her in the living area, he found her asleep on the chair, her neck bent at an uncomfortable-looking angle.

Poor thing. He had worn her out completely with their long trek through the jungle.

He sat on the other armchair, gazing out at the steady drumbeat of rain. How many of his turtles were nesting on Playa Hermosa during the last two nights he'd missed the egg count?

He should be upset at missing critical data, but somehow he couldn't summon more than a twinge of regret. He pondered that oddity. How had his life changed so completely in twenty-four hours? Two days ago, he would have been frustrated and angry at missing even one night's data, but somehow his priorities had shifted.

His work was important; he would never believe anything different. But right now this—ensuring Olivia's safety—was paramount.

He leaned his head back against the armchair and sat for a long time watching the rain and wondering how one small, stubborn, curvy female could walk into his life and shake it up so dramatically in only a handful of hours.

The contrast between the stress of the day and the quiet peace of this moment seemed to seep into his muscles and he closed his eyes, thinking he would only rest them for a moment.

He blinked awake some time later—not long, he saw when he checked his watch. He'd only drifted off for a half hour or so, but his neck still ached from the unnatural position and he imagined Olivia's probably was much the same.

It was silly for her to sleep out here when she could use the perfectly good bed in the next room. He went to her, more entranced than he had any damn right to be by the curve of her throat and a sweep of brown-blond hair across her cheek and the way she pursed her lips in her sleep, as if waiting for her prince's kiss.

He sure as hell was no prince, he reminded himself sternly. He was selfish and thoughtless and committed to his work to the exclusion of all else. A rich girl like Olivia Lambert should run as fast and as far as she could get from a man like him.

But not right now, when she needed to sleep. With gentle care, he scooped her into his arms, holding his breath that she would awaken. She only snuggled into him, wrapping her arms around his neck with a contented sigh.

Oh, she felt good. Warm curves and soft, sweet-smelling woman.

Olivia.

His breathing suddenly ragged, his heartbeat uneven, he wanted to stand there forever and just hold her, just absorb her female essence into all the hard edges of his soul, and he had to use all his self-control to force his muscles to move again.

The bedroom was dark, lit only by the pale, watery

moonlight reflecting off the white mosquito netting. He pushed it aside and lowered her to the bed. Her arms were still tightly wound around his neck so he had no choice but to follow her down to the mattress until he could extricate himself. She held on as tightly as a liana vine.

Bracing himself above her on one hand, he reached the other behind his neck to try to pry her free, all the while painfully aware of her curves pressed against him, her heat burning through the thin layers of her borrowed cotton dress.

He couldn't seem to break her hold from this awkward angle and the delectable feel of her body against his was quickly fraying the tenuous hold he had on his control.

"Olivia?" he whispered. "Sweetheart, you need to let go."

"Don't want to," she murmured, and tilted her head so her lips barely brushed along the side of his neck.

He closed his eyes, shivering at the raw heat scorching through him. She didn't know what she was doing; she was not even half-awake, he told himself. But somehow she managed to find exactly the right spot to fray that control even further.

Her eyes were open now, he could see in the moonlight filtering through the netting, just before she pulled his head down, seeking his mouth.

Like the rest of her, her mouth was soft and warm and tasted sweet and heady. Ren tried to hang on to sanity but the sudden glide of her tongue and the tangle of her legs around his were quickly eroding his control.

This was his only chance to touch her, to kiss her, some demon voice reminded him. Her father would be coming in a few hours, and then she would be out of his life, taking all this sweet eagerness with her.

He could surrender to the overwhelming temptation for just a moment without jeopardizing his control, he told himself. One tiny sliver of time. He would stop things before they went too far.

On a sigh, he kissed her, aroused beyond belief.

She gave a soft, erotic sound and responded with an enthusiasm that took his breath away, along with any vague idea he might have had about stopping anytime soon.

Their mouths tangled for long, delectable moments, until her body began to shift restlessly against him. Her borrowed dress buttoned up the front and it was an easy matter to work a few buttons free to reach silky skin beneath.

She wore nothing but the dress, he realized. He should have expected it since she had no change of underclothes except the bikini she'd been wearing on Suerte del Mar. Still, he felt a little jolt of shock at the sight of that creamy skin in the moonlight, at those lushly feminine curves that had haunted him from the moment he saw her.

"Touch me," she ordered, fully awake now, and he was helpless to resist. He wanted more light, wanted to see her laid out before him like some kind of gorgeous calendar girl from a different era. She was ripe and voluptuous and everything he had ever dreamed of in a woman.

He might have been able to resist her if that was her only appeal to him. But she was also brave and smart and funny and he was crazy about her.

She sighed his name, her hands massaging his shoulders, playing with his hair, exploring his skin.

They were going to catch fire in a moment, he was very much afraid. He tried frantically to hang on to his control, but it slipped further away with every touch of her mouth and caress of her fingers.

"Make love to me, Ren. Please."

He had to close his eyes against the heat and wild hunger thrumming through him. Though it just about destroyed him, he eased away from her.

"Olivia, I can't take advantage of you."

"What if I want you to take advantage of me?" she asked, her voice thready with need.

He groaned. "Liv—"

She cut him off effectively by wrapping around him again, until nothing in his world existed but her.

"You have to. It's my honeymoon."

A strangled laugh caught in his throat. "Wrong groom, babe."

"Who cares about him? He's a jerk who doesn't deserve me."

She smiled, but he saw lingering shadows in her eyes. He was quite certain her heart hadn't been bruised by her broken engagement. She had said as much at dinner. But perhaps her pride hadn't escaped unscathed.

He pressed his mouth to her forehead. "Damn straight, he doesn't deserve you. And neither do I."

She shook her head, sitting up against the headrest. In the moonlight, her eyes looked clear and alert, he saw with relief. At least he could put that worry to rest, that she was either still half-asleep or still mellowed from the wine.

"You saved my life, Ren. You protected me from all the snakes in the rain forest. Rafferty, the fer-de-lance, the squatters. All of them."

"You don't owe me anything for that. Especially not…this."

In answer, she leaned against him, all lush curves and sweet-smelling skin. He could feel her smile as she kissed him, though he thought perhaps it was a little on the tremulous side.

"I don't want to make love to you out of a sense of obligation. I want to make love to you because with you I feel things I had no idea I ever could. I need you, Ren."

How could any man possibly resist the entreaty in her vivid blue eyes, the low timbre of desire in her voice?

He had wanted her from the moment she brushed against him in the undergrowth of James Rafferty's estate, and every passing hour had only increased his desire.

She was every fantasy he'd ever had come to life.

And hell. He was only human.

"Please, Ren," she whispered again and he groaned as the lingering vestiges of his control flew out the window into the tropical night.

He yanked her to him again, his mouth urgent and demanding, and she responded with an exultant laugh that shivered down his spine like trailing fingers.

It was too late now. She had sealed her fate.

Something had changed. She could sense it in his kiss. One moment, he was restrained and cautious, the next he kissed her with a deep, urgent passion that took her breath away.

She gloried in it and wanted to absorb every touch, every kiss into her memory. Every sense was alive, hyperaccentuated. The rustle of the sheets beneath her, the lacy netting around them, the sound of the rain cascading outside. Everything seemed to add to her awareness of him.

He trailed kisses down her throat to her chest, bared after he worked the buttons free on her dress. She shivered when he kissed the slope of one breast and nearly swooned when his tongue darted out to lick and taste.

Her hands were busy taking his shirt off, baring those hard, broad muscles and all that beautiful skin. She caressed him, relishing the leashed strength she could feel there.

At last, when they had touched and explored until she was quivering with need, he leaned back and reached to pull off her sundress.

"I need to see you," he said, his voice roughened with desire. He flipped on the generator-powered lamp by the bedside and Olivia squirmed beneath his intense gaze.

She felt fat and uncomfortable and longed more than anything to pull the light blanket over her to hide her curves.

"You are absolutely the most beautiful thing I've ever seen."

"You don't have to say that," she mumbled. "I know I'm fat. It took me four months to lose fifteen pounds for the wedding and I think I've gained it all back stresseating in the last two weeks."

He leaned back, his eyes dark with unmistakable shock. "You're perfect, Olivia. I've been fantasizing about touching these curves since the moment I met you."

"You have not."

In answer, he arched an eyebrow and covered her curves with his fingers. "Have too," he murmured. "And I've fantasized about doing this."

She nearly came off the bed when his mouth moved to her breast and his tongue danced across her nipple.

"I've spent all day trying not to imagine all the ways I want to touch you."

She gasped as his fingers slid across her body to try out one of those methods in a particularly innovative spot.

His fingers danced at the apex of her thighs and she arched against him, forgetting all about feeling dumpy. Instead, more of that heady empowerment swept through her.

"For a scientist, you're amazingly creative," she managed to murmur through the heat scorching her.

"You have no idea," he murmured, his breath warm against her curves.

She wanted to find out, she thought. She wanted to spend all night in his arms, learning his secrets and sharing her own.

She had never felt like this, had never even imagined it was possible—this sweet surge of blood, the glittery tug on her emotions.

She wasn't crazy enough to think this meant anything more to him than a physical release after their ordeal together. She was not the sort of woman who could catch and keep a wild heart like Lorenzo Galvez.

In the morning she would catch a flight out of Puerto Jiménez for San José and then home. The heat and magic of this moment, the two of them entwined together while the rain poured down outside, might be all she ever had of him and it would have to be enough.

She pushed away the bittersweet thought and drew his mouth to hers for another of those drugging kisses as her hands explored his warm skin. She loved everything about him—the curve of his spine and the breadth of his shoulders and his slim hips.

His butt was a glorious thing. She should know, since she'd just spent all day watching it ahead of her on the trail. It seemed incredible that she was here in his arms and could touch everything she had watched and lusted over all day.

They spent long moments exploring each other, and then the mood seemed to shift. Everything took on a new intensity. His gaze roamed over her as he touched her intimately again, those clever, creative fingers playing across her sensitive folds.

At last, when she felt as if she stood on the edge of that jungle tree house ready to leap a hundred feet off into the unknown, he entered her. She gasped, wrapping her legs around him and holding him close, wanting to sear this moment into her memory.

His mouth met hers, his eyes burning with passion and something else, something soft and tender that took her breath away.

"Olivia—" he said, his voice raspy.

In answer, she arched against him, pushing him inside deeper. He groaned and gripped her hands in his, and their bodies tangled in a sensual tropical dance.

She forgot about being stilted in bed, about her usual discomfort and natural reticence. In his arms, she was a wild, earthy goddess and she claimed every ounce of her power.

She was back in that tree house in the rain forest, tee-tering on the edge, toes tingling and her stomach a jumble of glittery heat and need. He brushed his mouth against hers, and the silky rasp of his skin against hers sent her tumbling headlong over the edge, only to soar like one of those brilliantly plumed birds.

She gasped his name and his fingers tightened on hers, and then he joined her in flight.

She had no idea it was possible to feel so incredibly content, loose and comfortable inside her skin.

Ren pulled her closer until she laid half across him, his heartbeat a loud drumbeat in her ear. She traced a hand across the hard, defined muscles of his chest and wanted this moment to last forever.

He pressed a kiss to her forehead and Olivia closed her eyes, absorbing every sensation into her mind. She had never known this kind of intimacy, this soul-deep connection, had never even imagined it. And she certainly never guessed, judging by previous experience, that such fiery passion lurked inside her.

She might have never discovered such a glorious world if not for Ren Galvez, with his shaggy hair and wild edges.

Profoundly grateful for the twist of fate that had brought the orbits of their respective lives into a collision course, she kissed the hard line of his jaw. "Thank you," she murmured.

His laugh was rough and sexy and made her toes curl. "Oh, you're very, very welcome, Ms. Lambert."

"No, I mean it. I didn't…I've never…"

With a finger, he tilted her chin up and found her mouth again, his eyes almost black in the low light from the bedside lamp. She couldn't analyze the expression in them but something in it sent her stomach twirling again.

What could he read in her eyes? she wondered,

praying he couldn't see the emotions she was afraid were all too obvious.

"Are you hungry?" she asked. "I can fix you something."

He shook his head. "Maybe later. Right now, I don't want to move from this spot. This is perfect. You're perfect."

She snuggled closer, fighting the languor seeping into her muscles. She didn't miss the note of regret in his voice. He must sense, as she did, that these few stolen moments were all they would have together. When the sun came up, she would be on her way off the peninsula and out of his life. A lump of emotion rose in her throat, but she swallowed it.

She refused to ruin the moment by worrying about the future and the loneliness of a world without Ren Galvez.

"What will you do when you go back to the States?" he asked into the silence.

"Besides make sure Bradley Swidell is drawn and quartered? I don't know. I'm still considering my options."

She paused, then plunged forward. "I don't want to go back."

If she expected him to immediately offer her a spot on his research team, forever to cook him pasta and kayak across the Pacific with him, she was doomed to disappointment.

"You've got a tougher shell than you think, Liv," was all he said. "You can face all the gossip and furor over your engagement."

She decided not to correct his erroneous assumption. She didn't care anymore about the mess she'd left behind. She only regretted the idea of not seeing Ren again.

"I never thought I was. Tough, I mean."

"Are you kidding? I've never met a more resilient woman."

She tried the word on for size and decided she liked it.

"This trip hasn't turned out at all like I imagined," she admitted. "I thought I would soak up some sunshine, enjoy the local culture, maybe do a little long-overdue self-scrutiny. I landed in the middle of the rainy season and the only local culture I've seen has been monkeys and savage gold miners. Present company excluded, of course."

He smiled.

"Though I guess it's not a total failure. I did learn a bit about myself."

"Such as?"

"You're right. I'm tougher than I've always thought. And given the choice between climbing a hundred feet up a tree and sticking around on the ground with a deadly snake in the neighborhood, I'll climb any day."

He laughed out loud. "Knowledge I'm sure will come in handy back in Dallas. What else?"

She shrugged. "I don't know. I was a little too busy fighting off crazy turtle men with machetes to do much poking around in my psyche."

His fingers curved over her breast, his mouth twisting into a wolfish grin. "I think you lost the fight."

"Did I?" she murmured, and arched into his hand.

They made love again, without the wild urgency of the first time. This was slow and sensual, like drifting through warm, torpid tropical waters.

She came apart in his arms with the same bewildered kind of joy that rocketed right to his heart, then she fell asleep almost immediately. Ren held her for a long time as he waited for his pulse to slow and his breathing to return to normal.

An uncomfortable tenderness welled through him from some hidden spring.

She was different from any woman he had ever known, and he hated the idea of saying goodbye. Already he could sense the void she would leave behind, an emptiness that stretched ahead of him like the vast, undulating waves of the Pacific from Playa Hermosa.

He didn't want to think about it. Blast her, anyway. He wasn't looking for this. He had no room in his life for pampered little rich girls.

The rain had stopped completely, the moon sneaking from behind the clouds long enough to send a shaft of moonlight onto the almond-wood floor. He stared through the filmy netting.

Without the rain, he could hear the siren call of the sea, beckoning him as she had been doing since that long-ago summer in central California.

Suddenly restless, unwilling to face the tide of emotion crashing through him for this soft, curvy woman in his arms, he slid from the bed and threw on his shorts. Her cell phone sagged heavily in the pocket and he quickly pulled it out, guilty all over again.

He hadn't told her about calling her father yet. He'd tried half a dozen times but the words seemed to tangle in his throat.

He would wake her before daybreak to let her know, he told himself. How could he disturb the first real sleep she'd had in two days?

It was a rationalization, he knew. The truth was, he

didn't want to tell her, to ruin their last few hours together. She wouldn't be happy about what he had done. And while he couldn't regret calling her father— it was the one sure way to keep her safe and he would do it again in a moment—he wasn't quite sure how she would react.

Instead of dwelling on it, he yanked the cell phone out of his pocket and set it on her dress, then threw on a shirt and a pair of Tevas and let himself out of the beachhouse.

The night teemed with life. A chorus of smoky jungle frogs whooped to the accompaniment of cicadas and the loud, smacking kissy sounds of a pair of geckos as he made his way to the beach.

The lights of Puerto Jiménez gleamed down the shore and across the Golfo Dulce, he could make out the distant lights of Golfito.

He stood on the beach, watching the play of moon-light on the waves and listening to the night and trying not to think of how empty his life would feel when Olivia returned to the States.

He was in love with her.

It seemed impossible in such a short time but as he stared out at the sea, he knew he couldn't deny the truth.

He was in love with Olivia Lambert, with her strength and her spirit and her vulnerability.

Hell of a lot of good that would do him.

He let out a slow breath. He wasn't ready for this again. Mercedes's death had just about destroyed him. Not because he had loved her with a grand, never-to-be-repeated passion, though he had certainly cared about her.

More because it had starkly demonstrated what a selfish bastard he could be, not a pleasant realization for any man.

More than anything, he wanted to go back in time and live that day over—no, live the entire six months he spent with her again.

She had wanted him to take the day off. She was tired, she said. Not feeling well. They had been working sixteen-hour days for weeks without reprieve trying to finish their research, and she needed a rest.

He had berated her for it, he remembered now. Worse, he had accused her of trying to sabotage the project for her own petty reasons. It had been a vicious blow, completely uncalled for. She worked as hard as he did most of the time. Harder, sometimes.

She could have thrown the news of her pregnancy in his face then. That would certainly have shut him up in a hurry. It still surprised him that in the midst of one of their typically passionate arguments, she hadn't said a word and had let him kayak off with anger simmering through him.

She had known, he found out from a sister to whom she had sent an e-mail with the news. She had known for days that she was nearly three months pregnant and hadn't said a word.

Was that why she wanted him to stay home that day? If he'd stayed, would she have told him about the baby?

He didn't know, but he was almost certain that if he'd been there, he could have prevented the arsonists from burning down their research station. He hadn't been there. He'd been off nursing a snit while he collected data and then had gone to the cantina in Carate for a beer while Mercedes died from smoke inhalation, their unborn baby with her.

The real hell of it was, after the fire he had thought

long and hard about what his reaction would have been to the news of her pregnancy. He wanted to think he would have been thrilled, that he would have stepped up and done the right thing.

In truth, he just didn't know. He probably would have married her—his parents' example being what it was—but he had a feeling a marriage between them would have ended in disaster.

They had been lousy for each other in a lot of ways—competitive and self-absorbed professionally, and hot-tempered and reactionary when it came to their personal relationship.

After the needless tragedy of her death, he had figured things were easier if he packed that part of his life away. He planned to focus completely on his work and let that be enough for him.

He never expected a chance encounter with a bombshell in a bikini would completely turn his heart upside down, but there it was. Olivia Lambert had blasted her way through the hard shell around him, shattering it into a million pieces.

He was going to have a devil of a time piecing it back together when she left again.

He heard the sudden strident call of a vermiculated screech owl and sighed. He only had a few hours left with her. Why, exactly, was he out here on the beach moping about what he would do after she left, when he could be inside holding her right now?

He turned to go back to the bungalow, just as he heard the low throb of an approaching engine. Headlights suddenly turned up the road toward Al and Bobbi's house.

Two vehicles.

His heart sank and he picked up his pace. Her father was here already? He swore. To make it to Puerto Jiménez so quickly, Wallace Lambert must have already been in San José and chartered a plane.

Though he hurried, he was still thirty feet away when one of the vehicles—a Hummer—stopped and a man climbed out. He started to call out a greeting but some instinct stopped him.

The moonlight shifted suddenly, and every muscle inside him clenched in sudden dread.

That wasn't Wallace Lambert climbing out of that Hummer.

It was James frigging Rafferty.

Chapter 11

She awoke to a slow, languorous contentment.

She had no idea it was possible to feel so incredibly good. By rights, every muscle in her body should be aching right now. Instead, she was limber and relaxed, and she wanted this loose, easy feeling to last as long as possible.

A breeze whispered in through the open windows, sweet with the heliconia outside and a hint of the sea. The rain must have stopped sometime while she had slept because she could only hear the murmur of the ocean, soothing and peaceful.

She opened her eyes to find moonlight cutting across the room and the bed empty beside her. She stretched a hand out to the indentation on the other pillow and the linen was cool to the touch, indicating Ren had been gone some time.

A tiny, instinctive flicker of panic bubbled through her but she quickly pushed it aside.

He wouldn't have left her here alone.

She knew it with solid certainty. If he were the sort of man to abandon her, he could have done it anytime along their journey up to now, before he knew her at all.

She couldn't believe he would callously walk away after what they had shared.

A smile teased at the corners of her mouth as she touched his pillow again.

My word. She supposed the last few hours laid to rest any fears she might have harbored about being unresponsive and cold in bed. Her body stirred again, just remembering the heat and tenderness between them.

Three times.

She remembered her wild response and had to press her palms to her suddenly hot cheeks. She would have been mortified if Ren hadn't been just as wild for her. He acted as if he couldn't seem to get enough of her, and she couldn't quite get over her astonishment.

She pulled the empty pillow to her chest and dipped her head to inhale the scent of him lingering there.

She was in love with the man.

She let out a breath, unable to deny the realization. Her friends would be stunned and would probably call this some foolish infatuation. Just a natural reaction to a stressful situation, misplaced gratitude for a man who had saved her life.

It was more than that. She knew it with absolute certainty. The emotions poured through her like storm runoff cascading from a cliff.

She was in love with Lorenzo Galvez, marine biologist, adventurer and would-be rescuer.

He was strong and honorable, a man who would risk his own life to save that of a woman he had never even met. He was passionate about his work, about his family, about this unique and rare world in which he lived.

All those things were part of the reason she had developed feelings for him with such quicksilver immediacy, but they weren't the only reasons she loved him—or even the most important.

How could she do anything *but* love a man who could bring out such amazing things in her?

All her life she had felt inadequate, glaringly imperfect. A blond bimbo, just like her mother.

Ren didn't treat her that way. With him, she felt better, stronger, smarter. The Bionic Woman, only without the lithe figure, superacute auditory skills or the ability to twist a man to pieces with her bare hands.

When Olivia was with him, she felt as if she could do anything—climb a hundred-foot tree, fight off a pair of angry squatters, dye her hair, pose as a voluptuously pregnant villager.

Orgasm thrice in less time than it takes to paint her fingernails. She certainly never would have believed herself capable of *that*.

She covered her smile with her fingers, amazed at herself all over again.

She heard a door open somewhere in the bungalow, and anticipation swirled inside her.

Maybe he was hungry. She could warm up some of the pasta for him or throw something else together.

They'd never even made it to the gingered fruit waiting in the fridge.

She slid out from the mosquito netting onto the floor and reached for her borrowed sundress.

Something clattered to the floor—her cell phone, she realized with surprise. An odd place for it. Ren must have left it for her to find. She picked it up and slipped it into the wide pocket of her dress, then headed for the bedroom door.

It opened before she could reach for the knob. She smiled a greeting but it froze instantly on her features and she gasped a little scream.

"Stop right there."

The voice wasn't Ren's. Instead, it belonged to a strange man standing in front of her with a gun pointed at her heart.

She obeyed—what else could she do, with boneless knees and muscles that suddenly seemed locked into place?—and they stared at each other for a long moment.

He looked familiar, but she was certain she'd never met him before. Surely she would have remembered those cold blue eyes and the hard, handsome features.

She suddenly knew exactly who this stranger was. James Rafferty. She remembered his image from the magazine article Bradley showed her.

Her breathing quickened and panic spiraled through her as he inclined his head into the bedroom—a gesture not aimed at her, she realized, but at two large, intimidating men who stood behind him in the living area.

They obeyed instantly, moving with brusque alacrity past her into the bedroom. She was afraid to move—or even to blink, for that matter—but she could hear them behind her rummaging in the closet, the bathroom, even under the bed.

Where was Ren? she wondered frantically, but didn't have time to dwell on her worry. They didn't know either, obviously, or Rafferty wouldn't be ripping the house apart looking for him.

When the two men inside the room shook their heads at coming up empty, Rafferty dropped his weapon and advanced on her, his large features twisted into a solicitous expression.

"Olivia Lambert, I presume." He reached for her hand before she could shove it into her pocket. "Thank God we found you. You're safe now."

Her fingers clenched in his and she was certain he must feel them trembling. "I…I am?" she asked weakly.

"Where is Galvez?"

She would like to know that very thing, though she wasn't about to admit that to Rafferty.

She couldn't seem to make her brain work to come up with a convenient lie, so she decided it would probably be safer to stick to the truth. "I…I don't know," she finally admitted. "He was gone when I woke."

He swore sharply and viciously, his hand tightening on hers. "He could be halfway to Panama by now."

She had to hope so. Olivia had no desire to deal with James Rafferty alone, but she didn't want Ren to come charging in unarmed against the man and at least two of his thugs.

"What now?" one of the men asked in heavily accented English.

Rafferty made an impatient gesture. "Search the grounds. Just find him."

The men left swiftly, leaving her alone with Rafferty. Right then, she would have given anything to be back in the jungle, covered in mud and facing a dozen white-lipped peccaries looking for dinner.

"Did he hurt you, my dear?" Rafferty asked, still holding her fingers tightly.

He studied her for a long moment, and she could feel color creeping over her features. Oh, she hoped to heaven her lips didn't look as swollen as they felt, that she didn't have whisker burns on her skin.

"How did you find me?" she countered.

"Galvez called your father a few hours ago, demanding three million dollars for your safe return and giving the store down the road as a drop site. We were able to track your location from that brief phone call."

"He…he what?"

Her stomach roiled and she was suddenly hot and cold at once. Ren called her father and demanded a ransom for her? It couldn't be possible. He would never do that.

Still, enough doubt lingered that she had a hard time concentrating on Rafferty's next words.

"Your father promptly called me as he's still several hours away in Miami, and I have been acting as his representative here on the peninsula during the investigation until he can arrive himself. He's been sick about all this."

The room suddenly seemed to spin as her brain tried to work around both those possibilities. She didn't know which she found more far-fetched, that Ren would call her father or that her father would be at all worried about her.

"I…I need to sit down," she mumbled.

"Of course, my dear. Of course."

He led her to the couch and sat beside her, so close

she couldn't breathe for the smell of expensive cologne and Cuban cigars that clung to him.

Doubt began to creep in, vicious and demoralizing. How else would James Rafferty have found her, if Ren hadn't called her father? The odds that the gambling mogul would pinpoint their location so exactly, here in this secluded beach house on the coast, were too astronomical otherwise.

Three million dollars must have seemed an awfully tempting prize to a man who lived in a concrete research station and drove an old, beat-up Jeep.

Ren had changed after he found out she was an heiress. She couldn't deny that. All evening, he had been distant, distracted, and she had sensed something secretive and almost guilty in his eyes a few times when he looked at her.

Had he been after her money the whole time? Is that why he had made love to her, to divert her attention so she wouldn't pay heed to his actions or any mysterious phone calls he might make or receive?

It certainly couldn't be because he found himself suddenly overwhelmed with lust.

Rafferty squeezed her hands, and she didn't have to feign her shiver.

"I can't begin to tell you how much I regret that this horrible ordeal happened to you while you were my guest," he said. "Your father will be so relieved you're safe."

She made a noncommittal sound, trying not to burst into noisy, humiliated sobs.

"When you disappeared from my villa at the same time as Galvez, I have to tell you, I feared the worst. The man is a vicious criminal. An animal. I am sorry to have to tell you this, but two nights ago, he killed a guest at my villa, a lovely woman whose only crime was spurning his attention. When my men tried to apprehend him, he fled into the night. I was sick to learn another of my guests had disappeared at the same time. I have been moving heaven and earth to find you, my dear."

He certainly sounded convincing, with just the right notes of relief and concern in his voice. But at the starkness of his words, Olivia felt her sanity return.

He was lying. And poorly, too.

Ren would no more kill a woman who spurned him than he would start slaughtering sea turtles with his machete.

He wouldn't kill a woman and he wouldn't call Olivia's father demanding a ransom for her return. She was ashamed of herself for even entertaining the idea for longer than half a second.

The man who had rescued her from the squatters, who had teased and cajoled her through the rain forest, who had made love to her with such unmistakable tenderness, would never be capable of the things Rafferty was saying about him.

She didn't know how Rafferty had found them or what kind of game he was playing now, but she refused to believe Lorenzo Galvez would sell her out to her father.

As heartening as she found the assurance, renewed fear seemed to echo through her. *Where was Ren?*

Rafferty seemed to be waiting for an answer, an odd look on his features as if her reaction to his presence wasn't at all what he expected.

"I'm sorry you've been put to so much trouble," she

lied, trying to school her features into an expression of bubbleheaded relief. She couldn't underestimate Rafferty. He was clever and cagey and terrifying.

"You're safe now. I won't let anything happen to you." He slid an arm around her shoulder and again she had to fight a shudder.

"I can't tell you what a relief that is to hear," she said. Her limited acting skills just wouldn't stretch that far.

"You must come back to Suerte del Mar with me to await your father's arrival."

Alarm flashed through her. "Oh no. I'm sure I could wait here for my father."

"No, I insist on it." He smiled, but there was little warmth there. "It could be hours before he arrives. In the meantime, a warm bath and a safe bed will do wonders to put this ordeal behind you."

Why did he want her back on Suerte del Mar so badly? Whatever the reason, she had a feeling more waited for her there than expensive bath soap and an empty bedroom.

Panic spurted through her again. She knew she would have to be smart and resourceful to get through this.

Resilient. Wasn't that what Ren had called her? She could do this. No way was she placidly riding along beside James Rafferty, just quietly going along with the show. She was sick and tired of powerful men telling her what to do.

Not this time.

Biding for time, she decided to give him exactly what he expected. A blond cream puff, isn't that what he called her? If he wanted a cream puff, he would damn well get one.

Putting on her bimbo game face, she leaned into him so her breasts brushed his arm. "I can't believe my horrible ordeal is over at last." Her drawl thickened into her best effort at a distressed Southern belle. "I am so glad you found me, Mr. Rafferty. It was awful. Just plain *awful*. The things he made me do!"

"What things?" His eyes took on an avaricious gleam, and she didn't have to fake another shudder.

She grabbed at her hair. "Just look at this! It's hideous! He put this horrible stuff on it, some kind of berries or something to turn it black. I washed and washed it until my scalp was raw, and it still looks like some kind of bird flew over and took a big ol' crap all over it."

"It's not that bad."

"You are a sweet thing, aren't you? But you don't have to lie to me, Mr. Rafferty. I've seen a mirror and I know I look like death warmed over. I'm going to need a week of facials just to get my pores opened up again. And look at my poor little feet."

She held up her toes, with their raw blisters. That, at least, was a genuine complaint. "I can barely walk now after he made me tromp through that miserable jungle for hours and hours and *hours*. I thought I would never survive, let me tell you. And the mud. I have never seen such mud. It was everywhere! I had mud inside my ears. Do you have any idea how truly, horribly disgusting that is?"

She went on and on about the spa treatments she would need, how her cuticles were a complete mess, how the only thing he fed her was granola bars and beef *jerky*, for the love of Pete.

She threw in every complaint she could possibly

drum up against Ren Galvez. By the time she started to run out of steam and wind down her litany, Rafferty's eyes had started to cross.

"Yes, yes," he finally broke in. "You've been through a horrible ordeal, I'm sure, but it's all over now. I'll take you back to Suerte del Mar, put you into my loveliest room and you can wait there for your father."

A misnomer, his estate, she thought. She was afraid the luck of the sea would definitely *not* be with her if she stepped back there.

"Oh, thank you, Mr. Rafferty. Thank you, thank you." She added a little sob, hoping she wasn't laying it on too thick. No, she saw when she peeked out of the corner of her eye. He expected her to be Bradley Swidell's rich little blond bimbo and that's exactly what he saw.

"Let me just go use the little girl's room to run a brush through this mess of hair. I'll be right back, okay?"

He had the same glazed look her father tended to get when she was a teenager trying desperately to get him to pay a little attention to her and he looked almost relieved to have a reprieve from her inane chatter.

She closed the door behind her and turned on the water in the sink. The miserable boots were still in there from when she had showered earlier and she quickly shoved them on, not bothering with socks. Like the rest of the house, the bathroom had no screen on the window, just shutters that locked from the inside.

Maybe they wouldn't need so many mosquito nettings on the beds down here if they would invest in some screens, for heaven's sake, she thought, then yanked her wandering mind back to the issue at hand.

Praying she would fit—what could be more ignominiously humiliating than being stuck with her big fat butt hanging out?—she backed through the window, squeezing out feet first through the small opening.

Add this to her growing résumé of random skills, she thought, bordering on hysteria. She could squeeze like a tube of toothpaste through a bathroom window when the only alternative was dealing with a homicidal maniac.

She lowered herself down to the ground, muscles poised to take off running. Before she could make it a step, someone stepped out of the bushes and grabbed her from behind, a hard hand covering her mouth.

Good grief. She almost sighed. Hadn't she been through this already? She started to fight instinctively, then she caught a familiar scent on the tropical breeze.

"Shhh," Ren murmured into her ear, removing his hand from her mouth. "Rafferty has three men out here."

She stilled instantly, relief slamming into her so hard her knees swayed. As long as he was here, she could handle anything. She shifted so she could wrap her arms around his waist, hanging on with all her strength. He held her close and she thought she sensed the same relief in his embrace.

"They're looking for you," she whispered urgently. "You have to get out of here."

"Not without you."

He couldn't seem to stop touching her, amazed all over again that she'd had the strength and courage to climb out the window. He had never been so relieved in his life as he was to see those boots coming out the bathroom window.

He wanted to do nothing but stand here and hold her,

even though he knew Rafferty's men were scouring the vicinity for them.

"You'll be able to get away faster without me."

"Forget it, Liv," he said. "I'm not leaving you. We just have to elude Rafferty for a few hours until we can get in touch with Mañuel Solera when the sun comes up. That shouldn't be too hard. Stick close to me and we'll be okay."

She nodded and he wanted to hug her all over again.

"Just a minute," she said, "I have to tie my boots."

He waited while she tried, but her hands were trembling too much to work the laces. With a careful eye out for the three men he had seen skulking around the area, Ren knelt and quickly tied them, then grabbed her hand and sidled around the house using the lush landscaping to conceal their presence as best he could.

"How did Rafferty find us?" he asked when they were a dozen yards from the house, heading inland.

She gave an odd pause and he could hear her rapid, sharply defined inhalations. He moderated his pace slightly to give her time to catch her breath.

"He…he says you called my father demanding a ransom and gave the address of the *store* down the road."

He closed his eyes briefly. That damn phone call. He should have known Wallace Lambert would be in contact with James Rafferty. Rich white guys stuck together, didn't they?

Lambert would probably never have guessed that his daughter might ever be in danger from someone whose face had graced the cover of *Money* magazine.

"Did you?" she asked after a moment.

"Did I what?" he stalled.

"Demand a ransom?"

He snorted a laugh. "Hell no. Yeah, I called your father, but just to tell him where to find you. At this point, if I had three million dollars, I would gladly pay *him* to take you back."

She stopped dead in the cover of a huge purple jacaranda tree. "That was unnecessary."

He stopped too, stung by the pain in her voice. "Ah, hell. That's not what I meant. I just want you to be safe, Olivia. That's all. I'm not good at this, at being responsible for someone else. I'm doing a miserable job of it and I just can't bear the idea of anything happening to you."

He didn't miss the glare she aimed at him. "You're not responsible for me. I can take care of myself. I climbed out that window, didn't I?"

"You did," he answered, bringing his fingers to her mouth.

To his complete disbelief, he had to fight a smile. He was insane. He had to be.

It was three in the morning and they were on the run—again—from James Rafferty.

This time, he didn't even have the most basic of survival supplies, he had no idea where to take her and he wasn't sure what the hell they would do even after he told his story to Manny Solera.

He didn't care. She was here and she was safe, and for now, she was his.

It was the last thought flickering through his mind before he heard a sudden whoosh of air, had an instant of crushing pain. Then the world faded to black.

Chapter 12

At first, Olivia didn't know what had happened. One second Ren was arguing with her, the next he made a kind of strangled grunting sound and slid to the ground.

She thought maybe he tripped over a tree root or something, as she had done on the trail the day before. She reached to help him just as one of Rafferty's behemoths stepped out from behind the trunk of a tree, a hefty branch still outstretched in his hand.

"If you run, I will hit you next," he warned in gruff, heavily accented English.

He would drop her without a second thought, she knew. She wasn't going anywhere, though. How could she even consider trying to escape on her own, leaving an injured Ren behind to face Rafferty's fury?

With a hard glare to the thug, she knelt to ground where Ren lay motionless. He hadn't moved once since that hard crack to the head, she realized with a slick ball of dread churning in her stomach. That blow was hard enough to do serious damage.

"Ren? Can you hear me?"

She rolled him slightly. In the pale moonlight, his features were as still as death and he didn't respond at all when she nudged him.

She had a vague awareness of the man who had hurt him speaking tersely into a handheld radio but she was too wrapped up in her worry to pay much attention.

Moments later, Ren still hadn't stirred when a second hulk of a man stepped out of the jungle.

"You kill him?" Thug Number Two said. He was as big as the first man and blond—obviously not local talent.

"No, just hit him hard with this."

"I hope you haven't done too much damage. Rafferty has plans for this one."

Oh, she hated the sound of that. Though she longed to cover Ren's motionless form with her own, to protect him from these nasty men, she didn't have a chance.

"Take the girl," the light-haired one said. "I'll bring the crazy turtle man."

Before she could summon a protest, the man who had struck Ren lifted her from the ground without any apparent effort and started dragging her toward the bungalow.

She tried to dig her heels into the dirt, but she was no match against his muscles. Probably oozing with illegal steroids, she thought bitterly.

She tried to look back to see what was happening with Ren, but it was too dark and the man dragging her moved too swiftly.

"You be careful with him," she called back.

She heard low, amused laughter from behind her, but the man yanking her along like a pull-toy just moved faster. She had to run and stumble along to keep her arm from being yanked out of its socket.

She had screwed everything up. With her typical act-now, think-later strategy, she had blown it, big-time.

If she hadn't climbed out the window, Ren might have been able to escape on his own and she might have been able to fool Rafferty a little longer into thinking she knew nothing of the murder Ren had witnessed, that she was simply an innocent victim in all of this.

Rafferty said her father was on his way. She didn't know if she believed him, but if it was true, surely she could have stalled until he arrived with more of her bubbleheaded blond routine.

By climbing out the window, she had messed up that chance.

What kind of crazy hostage escapes from her rescuers—unless she knew she has far more to fear from the rescuers than from the man who took her in the first place?

Rafferty had to know by her escape that she had thrown her lot with Ren. She didn't care so much for herself, because she still couldn't quite believe he planned to kill her. But she hoped her escape didn't make things harder for Ren.

She had to figure out a way to get them both out of this. Ren had risked his life to extricate her from Suerte del Mar and she would gladly do the same for him. But right now, as the thug dragged her toward the front porch of the bungalow, she was running mighty low on ideas.

Rafferty was standing in the weak porch light of the

bungalow, looking urbane and sophisticated and slightly bored by the proceedings. She would have a difficult time believing he could murder a woman in cold blood, if not for the coldness in his eyes.

Her human handcuff dragged her up the steps to Rafferty and a moment later, the other man carried a motionless Ren up the steps and dropped him to the floor as if he were nothing more than a bag full of mulch.

She couldn't hold in her instinctive protest and she tried to move forward to check on him, but she couldn't budge the tight fingers around her wrist.

Rafferty no longer looked bored. It had been an illusion, she realized. Up close, she sensed that every inch of him seemed to simmer with fury. Still, his tone was incongruously polite. Solicitous, even.

"Ms. Lambert, I must admit, I'm baffled and hurt by your behavior. I've come a long way to rescue you, late at night and in poor driving conditions. I would have expected a little gratitude, rather than this pointless show of rebellion."

She had to bite her tongue to keep from telling him what he could do with his gratitude.

When she said nothing, Rafferty turned to his henchmen. "Tie him up," he ordered, in a voice as cold as an iceberg.

Olivia straightened. "I'm sure that's not necessary. He's unconscious, for heaven's sake!"

He hadn't stirred for going on three or four minutes now. That couldn't be a good sign.

Rafferty's smile didn't come anywhere close to reaching his eyes. "I have wasted far too much time these last few days trying to find you and your slippery

Señor Galvez to let you both escape again. This time, I'm afraid I'm taking no chances."

She had no choice but to stand by powerlessly while the blond behemoth bound Ren's wrists and ankles with a cord he produced from his pocket.

A moment later, one of the Humvees approached and a third man, just as massive as the other two, climbed out and helped the first man stuff Ren into the backseat.

"What about the girl?" The giant holding her wrist yanked her forward with a jerk.

Any semblance of civility from Rafferty disappeared. "Tie her up, too," he said, his voice cold.

He climbed into the front passenger seat of the Hummer without waiting around to see his orders carried out. Men such as him and her father didn't have to doubt they would be, she supposed.

A moment later, she was stuffed into the backseat next to Ren, trussed and terrified. She didn't know how much more adrenaline her body could manufacture without short-circuiting. Right now she wanted nothing more than to just curl up next to Ren's warmth and pretend everything would be okay.

She couldn't, of course. One of them would have to come up with a way out of this and since she was the only one conscious at the moment, she supposed the burden fell on her.

The other Humvee pulled out into the road first and they followed it just as the skies opened up again with another deluge. Good, she thought. Every moment longer it took them to reach Suerte del Mar was another moment she could try to figure out how she and Ren could escape.

They had tied her hands in front of her. With fingers that trembled in fear for Ren, she worked in the darkness trying to break free of the hastily knotted rope binding her hands.

Her fingers suddenly brushed something hard. The cell phone was still in the pocket of her dress. They hadn't bothered to search her or they would have found it. Now if only the two men in the front seat would become conveniently deaf, she could call for help.

No chance of that, she knew, so she did the only thing she could think of. After much maneuvering, she pulled it out of her pocket and concealed it with her bound hands.

From too many wasted hours talking to her girl-friends, she knew the workings of it by heart, and she knew just what buttons to push to silence its tones. Since she couldn't remember from her guidebook what emergency number to dial in Costa Rica, she did the only thing she could think of on the fly.

She hit Redial, hoping Ren had used her phone to call his friend at the police station.

"I'm confused about something, Mr. Rafferty," she spoke suddenly, praying someone was on the other end of the line to hear.

"What would that be, Ms. Lambert?"

"Why not just turn Ren over to the authorities in Puerto Jiménez? Why do you have both of us tied up in the back of a vehicle heading back to Suerte del Mar?"

That had to be a plain enough message for any self-respecting policeman, rural or otherwise. Manny Solera better be there and he better be hearing all this.

"He's a cold-blooded criminal," Rafferty said. "He must be brought to justice."

"I've heard about your brand of justice, Mr. Rafferty. Funny, but it's remarkably similar to my ideas of extortion and murder."

He laughed harshly. "I don't know what lies Galvez has been feeding you, but I would expect a woman of your age and experience to have a little better sense than to believe the word of a stranger."

"I trust Ren Galvez with my life."

"And hasn't that turned out well for you?"

"Say what you will, but I believe every word he told me about what he saw on Suerte del Mar."

In the dim green light from the dashboard, she saw him raise an eyebrow. "Please. Enlighten me. What did Lorenzo Galvez claim he saw?"

"Two days ago, you killed a woman over gambling debts, and Ren had the misfortune to stumble onto the crime. He also heard you sharing plans to provide a similar fate to another guest of your villa. When he bumped into me, he correctly guessed I was that ill-fated guest."

She prayed someone else was on the other end of the line, that they would get the message. At least if something happened to them, someone would know where to start looking.

After a long silence, Rafferty laughed. "My, my. For a scientist, Mr. Galvez certainly has a vivid imagination."

She had said almost those same words to Ren a few hours earlier when they were tangled around each other. The memory clutched at her heart and she had to take a deep, cleansing breath.

"I don't think so. I think my ex-fiancé owed you a considerable amount of money in gambling debts. I believe you planned to use me as leverage in some way to force Bradley Swidell to pay those debts."

"An amusing story, Ms. Lambert. Too bad you have no way of proving any of it."

"What are you going to do with us? Kill us? My father is a very wealthy, very powerful man. He's not some helpless, in-over-his-head gambler. I assure you, if I'm not returned to him completely unharmed, Wallace Lambert won't rest until he finds the truth about what happened to me. And the first person he'll go to for answers is you, Mr. Rafferty."

She thought she saw a flicker of unease in his gaze, but it disappeared quickly and she couldn't be sure in the darkness. When he spoke, his voice was cool and un-ruffled.

"You're not much of a gambler, are you, my dear?"

She almost laughed, thinking of how many times she'd spun the big old roulette wheel of fate in the last day. And she had sure poker-faced it just now with that big fat whopper about her father.

"I am," Rafferty went on without waiting for a reply. "And right now I have to play the hands I've been dealt. I fully intended to return you to your father this evening, earning his undying gratitude. Not a small thing from a man like Wallace Lambert and something I'm sure would have come in handy at some point in the future. But you had to ruin everything by climbing out that window."

Ren stirred suddenly beside her, and her attention was drawn away from Rafferty to him. Was he coming around? *Please, God, let him be okay,* she prayed.

When she wrenched her attention back to Rafferty, she sensed she had missed something important.

"It should be easy," he was saying. "I'll just make it look as if when I caught you both and tried to transport you to my estate to await police, Dr. Galvez tried to escape, killing both of you in the process. It will be tragic, really. You were so close to safety."

It was a terrible thing, to hear that death awaited her in the next few hours. She had to hope whomever was on the other end of the line heard the message. She glanced down at the concealed phone.

Nothing showed on the display. Absolutely nothing. The battery was dead, just like she and Ren would be now since her only brilliant idea didn't work.

A sob escaped her. What was she supposed to do now?

Ren stirred again. It seemed important that she conceal his slow return to consciousness from Rafferty and his thug in the driver's seat as long as possible.

The second time her sob was fake. She poured all her limited acting skills into it, all the while trying frantically to work the rope at her wrists free.

A soft sound of distress, like a small animal in pain, pierced the heavy fog enveloping him.

He wasn't in any big hurry to come back to full consciousness, certain on some instinctive level that when he did, he was going to hurt like hell.

Instead, he slowly became aware of random, disjointed impressions. A lurch in his stomach from steady movement, a strange ache in his wrists, leather upholstery against his cheek.

He heard a low murmur of voices in front of him and that distressing sound again, somewhere next to him.

He didn't want to open his eyes to face it. He wanted

to stay right here in this half-conscious state, at least until his stomach stopped these wild gyrations. But he couldn't block out that heartrending sound.

With mammoth effort, he pried open his eyes and nearly passed out again from the crushing pain in the back of his head.

He was in a vehicle of some sort, in the backseat, driving through the dark, he realized. It must be raining, and hard, too, by the sound of it thrumming against the car's roof and the rapid swish of the wipers.

For a long moment, he couldn't for the life of him piece together what he was doing in this vehicle and why his head felt like a coconut somebody had tried to crack with a steamroller.

Beside him, someone wept noisily. That was the noise he'd heard. It was too dark to see who it might be, and he wanted to tell whoever it was to shut up and let him think for a second.

He opened his mouth to growl the words, then a scent drifted to him, something clean and sweet and female.

Olivia.

In an instant, the events of the evening rushed through his head—waking with her tangled in his arms, the incredible rightness of it, walking down to the beach to try regaining a little much-needed perspective, then that gut-churning fear when he saw Rafferty going into the house.

He wasn't quite sure how they made it from that point to this, heading through the nightly rains in the backseat of a vehicle. He thought he remembered running through the jungle, trying to escape Al and Bobbi's *casita* but everything was a little fuzzy.

He only knew Rafferty had won, despite everything.

Olivia wept beside him and he moved restlessly, heedless of the pain in his head or the nausea in his stomach, conscious only of an overwhelming need to offer whatever small measure of comfort he could.

He made some kind of noise, but the sound died in his throat when she gripped his thigh with bound hands.

"Shhhh," she whispered, the command barely audible to him above the noise of the rain and the tires spinning in mud.

He frowned at that, even as he suddenly picked up a false note to her weeping. That impression was confirmed when his eyes became accustomed to the dark and he realized her fingers twisted and pried to work free the restraints on her wrists.

Clever girl! The crying was a distraction so neither Rafferty or his thug driving the Hummer paid much attention to the busy work of her hands.

He wanted to kiss her, a big loud smack right there in the backseat. He would have, if he didn't want to give the game away—and if the idea of it didn't make his head pound and the dizziness hover around the edges of his consciousness.

A moment later she made a tiny, triumphant sound and he saw through a sliver of moonlight that her hands were free.

Under the cover of darkness, she pulled his hands to her and started working on his restraints, keeping her movements subtle and easy so they didn't attract unwanted attention.

For once, the rain was a blessing, Ren realized. The driver was preoccupied with driving, concentrating hard on keeping the Hummer on the road. Rafferty growled commands to the driver, apparently not content to just sit passively in the passenger seat.

Ren shouldn't be passive, either. He needed to figure out some way to get them out of here. Focusing on the problem at hand wasn't an easy task, especially when his brain felt as slow and sluggish as one of his Ridleys on dry ground.

It also didn't help his powers of perspicacity to have Olivia so close, her hands smooth and cool on his and her clean, sweet scent filling all his senses, until he only wanted to lean into her, close his eyes and inhale.

Was she making progress? He couldn't tell much in the dark, but he was certainly enjoying her efforts.

If she did get his hands free, what next? He could probably overpower Rafferty—though in his queasy, head-pounding state, he wasn't a hundred percent certain of that. But even then, he'd still have the beefy driver to contend with. Either or both of them was probably armed, which complicated everything.

He was considering his options when the Hummer, going much faster than he was comfortable with in the dark and in the middle of the heavy rains, suddenly slid sideways in the mud and started heading for the side of the road and the steep hills below.

The driver hit the brakes much harder than he should have under the circumstances—a couple good taps were far more effective in a slide—and one of their tires actually hung over the side. He eventually regained control and brought the SUV back to the middle of the road.

"You idiot!" Rafferty yelled when the immediate danger had passed. "Are you trying to kill us all?"

"I can't think with all that blubbering," the other man complained.

Olivia returned her hands to her own lap a fraction of a second before Rafferty turned around to glare at her.

"Enough with the crying," he growled. "It's a miracle Galvez didn't throw you off a sea cliff just to put himself out of his misery!"

In answer, she sobbed louder. Even though Ren knew she was manufacturing the tears, he had to fight the urge to reach for her.

"I mean it," Rafferty snarled. "Shut up."

"I can't help it," she sniffled.

"Figure out a way or I'm going to shoot you here and dump you into the river for the alligators."

"What difference does it make if you kill me here or kill me at Suerte del Mar? I'm dead either way."

Ren held his breath at her defiance, watery though it was. *Don't push him too far,* he thought, but he was stuck beside her playing dead and could say nothing.

Rafferty suddenly pulled out a gun, dull and black and deadly, and Ren froze, his heart racing and fear pulsing through him.

Olivia apparently was far more sanguine than he. Her chin lifted. "Go ahead. Shoot me," she said. "I don't care."

Ren wanted to groan. A man who could build a billion-dollar gambling empire in only a few years wasn't the sort likely to back down from a challenge.

He didn't know whether to cover her with his own body or shove her out the damn door.

"Here's a better idea," Rafferty drawled. "How about you stop your whining or I'll shoot the scientist."

Olivia drew in a sharp breath and reached for his hands blindly. Before Ren could even react, Rafferty swung the gun in his direction. He heard a sharp pop and Olivia screamed.

Chapter 13

The acrid smell of burnt leather and gunpowder filled the interior of the Hummer. Olivia threw herself across his chest, sobbing in earnest now.

With his wrists bound and trapped between their bodies, Ren could do nothing but lean his cheek on her hair and gaze at the tiny plume of smoke spiraling from a hole in the leather seat, just three or four inches from his head.

"You missed," he drawled. His voice sounded rusty, strangled, but he still managed to get the words out.

Rafferty laughed. "I figured that would wake you up. Or at least get you to stop faking being out of it. Looks like it worked."

"Waste of perfectly good leather, if you ask me."

His teeth gleamed in the darkness in a feral smile. "We do what we have to do. Feeling better?"

He shrugged and then had to fight a wince as the slight

movement sent an army of jackhammers pounding cheerfully away in his brain. "Can't complain."

Rafferty laughed again. "I always liked you, Galvez. You're one crazy son of a bitch but you've got titanium *cojones*."

He wasn't sure anyone could consider that a compliment, coming from a man who had just fired a Sig Sauer into his own upholstery. "We do what we have to do," he parroted.

Olivia's cries had dwindled to sniffling sobs but she didn't seem in a hurry to move. Her hands were fluttering between them in the vicinity of his lap, stirring up all kinds of inappropriate reactions, given the circumstances.

It took his befuddled brain a full minute to realize she was only continuing her efforts to untie the rope around his wrists, too bad for him.

Rafferty studied them. "You two certainly look cozy. Am I missing something here? I thought Ms. Lambert was supposed to be on her honeymoon. And with quite a different gentleman, if I'm not mistaken."

Olivia slid away and Ren realized his hands were now free as well, the rope draped loosely around them for appearances in case Rafferty or his driver took a yen to look closer.

"Bradley Swidell is no gentleman," she said, her voice low. "He owes you money, doesn't he? And lots of it."

"I'm afraid I don't bandy about the names of those with accounts outstanding at any of my online operations. Discretion is so important in my particular business. I'm sure you understand."

The bastard was enjoying this, Ren thought. He savored having them at his mercy—and loved even more that they knew it and were helpless to do anything about it. Rafferty reminded him of a jaguar playing with its prey, tossing it from pad to pad until it tired.

Olivia wiped at her eyes and Ren could almost see her straightening her spine, vertebrae by aching vertebrae. He couldn't understand how she could ever consider herself a wimp. She was quite possibly the strongest woman he had ever met.

"Bradley promised to pay you from my trust fund after we were married, didn't he?" Her voice was restrained but firm. "That's why he insisted we come to Costa Rica on our honeymoon, so he could flaunt me in front of you and prove to you the deed was done. I was his golden egg."

Rafferty gazed out the window for a moment as if debating what to say, then turned back around to face to them. "I suppose there's no reason not to tell you now."

Ren did *not* like the sound of that, though it came as no surprise to him that Rafferty believed anything he said now would go with them to their graves.

"You're absolutely right," he went on. "Your intended groom owes me a considerable amount of money. One-point-two million dollars."

Olivia inhaled sharply at the amount and Rafferty smiled that devil smile.

"As we both know, you are worth far more than that. When he found himself in…difficulties, Mr. Swidell promised to hand-deliver a check once he was married to you. I took him at his word. More fool, me. Then you showed up at Suerte del Mar alone and I learned to my considerable chagrin that the wedding was off. Not only would Mr. Swidell not be accompanying you to Costa

Rica but, more importantly, he would not have access to the money he promised me. As you can imagine, I was not pleased."

"Completely understandable. He broke his word." She spoke with impressive calm, under the circumstances. "But why take it out on me? I've never gambled a dime at your casinos. I didn't do anything but break an engagement that never should have happened to a rat fink who never should have been born."

"I regret any inconvenience to you, but Swidell needed to be taught a lesson." Rafferty smiled coldly. "I assure you, I wouldn't have killed you, my dear. With your wealth and your father's position, you're not exactly disposable like some nameless woman from Iowa. I only intended to extend your stay at Suerte del Mar a little longer than you planned."

"You intended to kidnap me and hold me for ransom until Bradley paid up," she said flatly.

"Something like that. But Dr. Galvez beat me to it and kidnapped you first."

For the first time, her voice rose. "He didn't kidnap me. He rescued me from you."

Warmth and something much deeper, soaked through Ren as he listened to her defense of him.

"Ah yes. Dr. Galvez and his vivid imagination again."

"It's not my imagination," Ren finally interjected. "I know what I saw. You killed that woman, Jimbo."

Rafferty's jaw tightened. "Which brings up an interesting question I've been wondering about for two days. What exactly were you doing trespassing on Suerte del Mar the other night, Dr. Galvez?"

He didn't want to answer. The truth seemed so banal

after all they had been through since he'd stumbled onto that grisly scene.

"My turtles," he finally said after a long pause. "Your dogs were harassing the nesting sites again. This time I had pictures. I came to warn you I was planning to plaster them all over the Internet if you didn't do a better job containing your Dobermans."

Rafferty stared at him for a full twenty seconds, then started to laugh. "This whole thing started because of a couple of dogs and some stupid turtles? What lousy timing on your part."

His laughter faded as abruptly as it started and even in the darkness, Ren could see his eyes turn cold. "One would have to say it was in the nature of a fatal mistake."

Olivia grabbed his hands again, her nails digging into his skin, and Ren was overwhelmed with the onus of responsibility. He couldn't regret that night, taking her from Rafferty's estate. Despite the man's claims that he wouldn't have hurt her, Ren had a hard time believing she would have emerged unscathed at his hands.

James Rafferty wasn't noted for his self-restraint. And thanks to her idiot of a fiancé, he had one-point-two million dollars worth of reasons not to treat her with kid gloves.

That vivid imagination Rafferty accused him of having unfortunately could devise plenty of ways this man might harm a vulnerable woman who found herself completely at his mercy.

Ren knew there was no sense dwelling on those things, on what might have happened if he hadn't stumbled across her— especially when he was grimly aware that Olivia was probably in far worse danger now than she would have been if he had simply left her to Rafferty in the first place.

Rafferty had nothing to gain now by keeping them alive and everything to lose.

It was up to Ren to figure out a way to put the odds firmly back in their favor.

His head ached like a mother but he unobtrusively turned his attention out the window to try to catch his bearings.

On this isolated, sparsely populated coast of the peninsula, it was difficult to find landmarks in the dark, but he finally saw an old abandoned shack he recognized. They were only about two miles from Playa Hermosa, with Suerte del Mar just a few miles beyond that.

They didn't have much time. He knew once they rode through the gates of Rafferty's estate—where his word was law and everybody was armed, from Rafferty himself to the lowliest maid—there was a damn good chance they would never make it back out.

If they were going to escape, they would have to act soon.

They would have to run for it again. She had been through so much and he knew she was physically nearing the end of her endurance. He could only pray she could wring a little more out of herself and that he had the physical fortitude to push himself, as well.

He tried to figure out their options, factoring the topography and any elements that might come in handy for their escape.

Suddenly he straightened with excitement as an idea came to him. It wouldn't be easy, but right now he couldn't come up with anything else. With the right combination of circumstances—and a hell of a lot of that *suerte*—they just might make it.

"Did the sugar daddy pay up?" he asked, trying to keep Rafferty talking and distracted while he went to work on the restraint at his ankles and gestured for Olivia to do the same.

"Excuse me?"

"That woman I watched you kill. Was it worth it? Did the man with her pay his debt?"

"I had a check within the hour." He spoke with smug self-congratulation that Ren found obscene, considering the circumstances. "I regret I had to take such drastic measures but her *sugar daddy*, as you call him, left me no choice. For weeks, I warned him he would face dire consequences if he didn't make some attempt to pay his debts. Tommy Bialetti owns a string of very lucrative car dealerships in the Midwest. He was more than capable of paying what he owed, he simply chose not to. After several more traditional debt collection measures failed, I had to show him an honorable man does not walk away from his obligations. I believe he got the message, don't you?"

"Do you really think you'll get away with it? Killing her, killing us? That is what you plan, isn't it?"

"Like Tommy Bialetti, you've left me very little choice, I'm afraid. And no, I don't anticipate any ramifications once I've dealt effectively with the two of you."

"What about my father?" Olivia asked.

Ren quickly ascertained she had removed her ankle restraint and was drawing Rafferty's attention to her so Ren could work more aggressively on his own.

"He will want answers," she went on, "and I'm afraid

your convenient little botched-rescue scenario isn't going to wash with a man like Wallace Lambert."

Rafferty's jaw tightened. "I will simply have to make the evidence indisputable, won't I?"

"You'll have to do better than that. My father won't rest until he finds the truth about what happened to his cherished only child."

"Is that right? According to our mutual friend Mr. Swidell, your father considers you more in the nature of an inconvenience and was delighted to turn over responsibility of you to his trusted associate. *A perpetual disappointment* were Bradley's words, I believe."

She stiffened, drawing in a harsh breath. Direct blow, Ren thought. He cursed her father, and he cursed Rafferty for rubbing salt in that particular wound. Most of all, he cursed Bradley Swidell for putting her in this predicament in the first place.

They were nearing a bad section of the dirt road, a natural drainage channel where runoff from the hills on the inland side of the road cut across to wash down to the sea. It was muddy and slick and particularly treacherous here, with a steep drop-off to the Pacific.

On either side of the road was thick, nearly impenetrable growth. *Nearly* impenetrable, but not completely, not for someone like him who knew this area well.

As he expected, the Hummer had to slow down to negotiate the mud, though the driver was still clipping along at a moderate pace.

When Rafferty's attention was diverted by haranguing the driver to slow down further, Ren grabbed Olivia's hand and gestured to the door. He made a swooping little gesture with his hand to indicate what he wanted them to do. In the darkness, he could see the whites of her eyes as they widened. She shook her head with a hard, brisk movement.

He tugged her hand a little more insistently and was again overwhelmed with her trust in him when she let out a hard breath through her nose, then nodded tightly.

He judged his spot just right, gripped her hand tightly in his and prepared to jump out into the unknown.

This was insane. *He* was insane.

Crazy turtle man.

Olivia had just an instant to wonder if she would rather die from jumping out of a moving vehicle or die at the hands of James Rafferty. Before she could puzzle that out, in a blink Ren shoved open the door and leaped out.

The Hummer wasn't going very fast in the mud, but jumping out of it still knocked the breath out of her.

He didn't even give her a second to scramble for it again before he half dragged, half carried her into the dark, murky forest.

"Are you hurt?" Ren asked.

She shook her head, working hard to suck oxygen into her lungs. Behind them, she could hear shouts and curses and the sounds of rapid pursuit. He had his fingers clamped hard around her wrist as if afraid to let her go. She had no choice but to try to keep up with the bat-out-of-hell pace he set for them.

"Come on, babe. We won't have much of a head start. All we've got is that minute or two element of surprise. Rafferty's going to be right behind us. We've got to haul it here."

She couldn't believe they were out of that vehicle—

nor could she believe she was actually being forced to run for her life through the blasted jungle again.

Ren seemed to be going in no discernible direction—cutting across a stream here, over a rock here. But since their way was relatively unobstructed by the thick growth, she assumed he must be following a vague trail.

"What's our plan here?" she asked, when she decided the immediate danger of hypoxia had passed.

He looked around him as if gauging their whereabouts. Since she couldn't see a darn thing through the darkness and heavy rain, she decided he either had eyes like a puma to see in the dark or he was suffering the lingering effects from his head injury.

"You're not going to like it," he finally answered.

"As long as it doesn't involve a slow, torturous death at the hands of a psycho like James Rafferty, I'm game for anything."

Unbelievably, he stopped on the trail, his dark eyes glittering in the moonlight.

He had to be crazy, she thought again.

Rain was pouring down on both of them, it had to be 4:00 a.m. or later, armed, dangerous men were hot on their trail and he had a damn head injury, but Dr. Lorenzo Galvez didn't seem to want to do anything but stand there grinning at her.

He was crazy.

And she was crazy in love with him.

"You are one hell of a woman, Olivia Lambert."

She shook her head, though for the first time in her life she was beginning to believe it.

"So what are we looking for?"

"Nothing now. Here we are. Take off your dress."

She blinked. "Excuse me?"

"That sundress thingy. You're going to have to take it off."

"I can't! I'm not wearing anything underneath!"

"Really?" That seemed to divert him momentarily from the crisis at hand, but he quickly jerked his attention back. "I'm sorry, sweetheart, but you'll break your neck if you try to climb in that."

Sudden dread pumped through her. "C-climb where?"

He pointed to the tree next to her. "It's not nearly as far as the tree house. There's a platform here, only about twenty or thirty feet up."

She saw the climbing rungs then and couldn't believe he was going to make her do this again.

Terror threatened to overwhelm her but even as she stood there in petrified indecision, she could see the beam of flashlights cutting through the trees as their pursuers approached.

"Come on, Liv," Ren said urgently. "We have to."

She couldn't let Rafferty win. He would kill both of them and she would have no one to blame but herself. Instead of taking her dress all the way off, she quickly gathered up the hem and tied the edges into a hard knot just below her posterior to keep her legs free, drew in a deep breath for courage and grabbed hold of the bottom rung.

The next few minutes were a hellish blur. She ignored the ache in her arms, the scrape of bark against her bare skin, the gut-churning fear. All she could focus on was finding the next rain-slicked rung in the darkness and hauling herself ever upward.

Below, she could hear shouts and calls among Rafferty's men but she didn't dare risk looking down to see if they had seen the tree.

At last, when her muscles were quivering and she was afraid she couldn't go another foot, she reached a small wooden platform, perhaps five feet by seven feet. She pulled herself up and flopped to her back, her pulse pounding and her breathing ragged.

Ren was right behind her. He joined her on the platform, his breathing just as labored. For several long moments, they lay without moving. Then he reached for her and held on tight.

"Please don't make me do that again," she begged.

"I won't, baby. I promise."

He kissed her forehead and then tilted her chin up so he could slant his mouth over hers. His lips were salty and cool from the rain, and in his arms she felt safe for the first time since Rafferty walked into their bedroom back at the beach.

"I'm sorry, Liv." He whispered the words in her ear and she was reminded there were armed men looking for them thirty feet below. "I'm so sorry I called your father. I honestly thought it would be the best way to keep you safe. I never for a minute would have guessed he would go straight to Rafferty with our location."

She had forgotten the phone call that had set the events of the last hour in motion. She shook her head at the guilt in his voice. "You couldn't have known. I never would have suspected it, either."

"If I hadn't called your father, Rafferty would never have figured out where we were."

"And if I hadn't been stupid and stubborn enough to

go on my honeymoon by myself, I never would have been standing on that trail at Suerte del Mar."

She would have been safe in Fort Worth with no idea that somewhere else in the world lived a crazy turtle scientist with warm brown eyes and unshakable courage.

If not for Ren, she would have spent the rest of her life trying to measure up to her father's unreachable expectations, never guessing at the deep reservoir of strength inside her.

She would have been miserable.

"How's your head?" she whispered.

She felt his shrug and to her regret, he released her and sat up. "Still feels like I went a couple dozen rounds with the heavyweight champion of the world. What did that ape hit me with?"

"Tree branch. You went down hard."

"And took a trip to the Bahamas for a while, apparently."

"Why would you need to go anywhere else, even when you're unconscious? We're already in paradise, right?"

He laughed softly at her dry tone and kissed her hard again, then moved around to explore their platform.

"What are you doing?" she whispered. With every movement, their perch swayed dangerously.

"We can't stay here all night. You're shivering."

"I'm afraid of heights, remember?"

He grinned at her again. "Yet here you are anyway. Like I said, you're one hell of a woman, Olivia. I would love to stay here and give you time to rest but sooner or later, Rafferty and his men will see the rungs."

"How did you find them in the darkness and know they led to a platform?"

"I helped a buddy build it last summer in exchange for some work he did on my research digs."

"Is he a scientist too?"

"Nope. Fisherman. He needed a quick way to get down to the beach and this is what we came up with."

She frowned. Before she could make sense of that, she heard voices below.

"Boss, I found something," a voice called out.

"What are you waiting for?" Rafferty responded. "Go check it out."

Ren cursed. "Okay. We have to go."

"Go where?" she exclaimed. "We can't climb back down now without meeting Rafferty's goon headed up."

He grabbed her and hauled her to feet and led her to a corner of the platform that was missing the railing that surrounded the rest. For one crazy moment, she thought he meant for her to jump; then he handed her something.

A zipline, she realized. It was the trolley to a zipline leading off the platform and heading down to the Pacific. Her heart started that wild staccato rhythm again.

"Just hang on tight to this, okay? You'll come out right on the beach, on soft sand. There's nothing to be afraid of. It's only about six hundred yards and it's perfectly safe."

"I can't do this, Ren. I can't!"

"Yes, you can! You can do *anything*. I can stall the guy coming up for a minute or two, but I can't keep them all from climbing after us. Sooner or later we're going to have to fly out of here. There are only two trolleys, so they can't come after us, at least without taking the hard—and I mean hard—way down. It's the only way, Olivia."

She knew he was right but that didn't make what she had to do any easier. Still, she had made it this far. She could come up with enough adrenaline to push her through this, too.

She grabbed hold of the handles. "Ready?" he whispered. She could hear Rafferty's thug climbing ever closer.

"Yes," she lied, then swallowed a scream as the man she loved gave her a hard push into nothingness.

After the first shock, she almost laughed at the sparkly sensation of flying through the air tethered only by a narrow steel-gauge zipline. It was exactly like being in his arms, she thought. Wild and exciting and incredible.

Her borrowed sundress was flying out behind her and she could only be glad it was dark and no one could see her mooning the world. Still, the cheery yellow color of her dress must have attracted some attention below. After just thirty seconds or so, she heard yelling and cursing, followed instantly by several sharp pops.

Rafferty was shooting at them, the bastard. She held her breath, her arms being pulled nearly out of their sockets, until she left the shooting behind her. A moment later, the beach rushed up to meet her. She landed with a hard oomph and only had time to roll out of the way before Ren hit the ground right behind her.

"Did they hit you?" he asked urgently.

"No. I'm okay."

He yanked her into his arms. "We did it! I can't believe we made it."

He kissed her hard again, with a fierce, radiant joy. As she savored the taste of him and the wild fluttering of her heart, she thought she would be willing to do just about anything for that kind of reaction.

Probably not a good idea to share that little tidbit of information with him, she decided, given the things he had asked of her up to now.

Chapter 14

He stepped away far too quickly. "Cesar keeps his boat over down the beach a little ways. Just keep your fingers crossed that it's got enough fuel to get us to Golfito."

She followed him down the beach. "Not Puerto Jiménez?"

"I think that's our best option now. As soon as he figures out we're taking to the ocean, Rafferty will be watching the beaches in Port J. He won't leave us any safe place to come ashore."

The boat he talked about was small—probably no bigger than sixteen or eighteen feet long, with an outboard motor. And he expected them to take that all the way to Golfito? She supposed it was probably better than a kayak, but not much.

"Can you help me drag it down to the surf?"

She grabbed hold and tugged with her aching arms.

When they reached foaming surf, he came over to her side of the boat. "I'll help you inside, then tow us out a little way."

Compared to everything else she had done for him, this seemed a small thing but the idea of being out in the ocean in this small craft that smelled of fish and tobacco was terrifying. But already she could hear shouting and crashing through the brush as Rafferty's men tried to reach them.

She drew in a breath and once more placed her hand in his. He lifted her into the boat, then tugged it through the water to deeper surf. When they were perhaps a dozen feet from shore, he climbed in and went to work on the motor.

To Olivia's vast relief, it fired up a moment later with a low, powerful throb.

"Here we go. Hang on!" In the moonlight, she could see his grin and her heart seemed to turn over in her chest.

How could any woman not love a man like this, someone strong and gorgeous, who thought she was re-silient?

The small boat had a kick-butt motor, and they were soon some distance from the beach.

The moonlight was stronger now as the clouds had passed over, and in its pale glow, she could see three men reach the shore behind them. The darkness and distance obscured their features, but she thought one raised a weapon and fired it.

She shivered, exceedingly grateful they were out of range.

That made three times now people had shot at her—four, counting the police that first night—and it wasn't an experience she cared to repeat anytime soon.

Ren laughed out loud as they motored away. "We did it!" he exclaimed over the throb of the motor. "Now we just have to find our way around the peninsula to Golfito and we're home free."

She smiled in response but the outboard was too noisy for much conversation.

It was cool out here on the water, especially since she wore nothing but a rain-soaked sleeveless dress. She folded her arms across her chest and rubbed her shoulders.

Ren gestured to the wide bench behind them. "See if you can find a couple life jackets," he yelled. "Cesar might even keep a blanket or two in there."

She didn't feel a hundred percent comfortable moving around on a small fast-moving boat like this—it would be just like her to topple over the side when Ren hit a wave or something—but she managed to maneuver so she was kneeling on the bottom of the boat, still relatively stable, while she lifted the hinged lid of the storage bench.

Inside, she found a couple of orange life jackets. She handed one to Ren, then slipped the other over her dress. Deep in the interior of the storage bench, she found a wool blanket that smelled of gasoline and salt water. She didn't care; she was just grateful for the warmth as she wrapped it around her shoulders.

This was the first time since she landed in Costa Rica that she didn't feel as if she were slowly simmering in her own juices. It seemed an odd sensation, to be cool, bordering on cold.

She snuggled into the blanket, suddenly exhausted from the strain of the last few hours. She had only caught a few hours' sleep back at the bungalow before James Rafferty burst in on her.

The combination of the blanket's warmth and the steady hum of the motor—not to mention the release from the overwhelming terror that she and Ren might not make it through this—sent a pleasant lassitude soaking through her exhausted muscles.

Despite her efforts to prop them open, her eyelids drooped and she huddled down into the seat.

"Lay down," Ren called. "There should be room. We've got a two-hour boat ride, so you might as well get some rest."

She wanted to stay awake but her exhausted, achy body ruled against her. As her adrenaline crashed, she could do nothing but curl up on the seat facing Ren, tug the blanket over her shoulders and drift away on the tide.

From his spot at the wheel, Ren watched Olivia's eyelids flutter a few times, then go still.

Good. She deserved a rest. He wished he could give her silk sheets and yards-thick mattresses instead of a scratchy old army-issue blanket and a hard metal bench, but at least she was safe.

The alternative didn't even bear contemplating.

He knew they'd had a lucky escape. If not for Rafferty's thugs and their careless knot-tying, he and Olivia would probably be dead right now. Hell, they could have been dead a dozen times on this crazy ride they'd been on for the last two days.

He was not a man who believed in miracles—give him cold, hard science any day—but he couldn't deny they had either been extraordinarily fortunate or someone had been watching out for them.

He kept one eye on the dark outline of the shore and the other on the vast ocean ahead of them.

They weren't safe yet. He still had to negotiate miles of ocean to Golfito and then find a way to contact Manny. His head still throbbed in synch with the engine's growl, though he wanted to think the ferocity of his headache had eased a little.

For the first time since he'd seen James Rafferty standing outside Al and Bobbi's bungalow, Ren allowed himself hope.

It seemed a lifetime ago that he had held her in his arms back in that netting-draped bed.

He settled back on the seat and gazed at her sleeping form. In sleep, she looked soft and vulnerable, like a bedraggled little girl lost in the wilderness. He wanted to lift her onto his lap and hold her close until she found her way again.

She was amazing.

She deserved the credit for their escape far more than he did. She had been the one to work free of the cords binding her wrists, which enabled her to help him do the same. Without that small act of providence and ingenuity on her part, they would right now probably be alligator food.

He thought of Rafferty's words that first day at Suerte del Mar. Ren hoped the man had figured out by now how he had severely underestimated the cream puff he thought would be easy prey.

There was more to Olivia Lambert than Ren would have guessed—and far more than he thought she herself realized.

She was clever and sweet and unbelievably brave. A

hundred times over the last few days, he had seen her face her fears and shove right through them. She had done every impossible task he asked of her and then some, with a faith and trust that humbled him.

The terrified, white-faced woman he had taken at machete-point had spread her wings and become like one of the morpho butterflies that flitted through the rain forest.

He was in love with her.

He inhaled sharply at the ache in his chest. All his efforts at keeping her out of his heart had come to nothing. She had wiggled her way in regardless of his defenses.

What the hell was he supposed to do about it?

He sighed. Nothing. He could do nothing. Once they reached Golfito and reported what had happened so Rafferty could be arrested, they would go their separate ways. She would go back to Texas and he would go back to his turtles.

The thought held no appeal to him right now. Already his stomach twisted at the idea of saying goodbye.

His life—the world that had seemed so satisfying, so meaningful, the day before yesterday—would be cold and barren without Olivia Lambert in it.

He could handle that. He had practice at stumbling through the motions of life when it felt as if fate, like Rafferty's goon, had smacked him in the head with a good stout tree branch. While he did not look forward to their inevitable parting, what he dreaded most was that she would return to Texas and leave behind the bright, iridescent wings she had found here.

He didn't know the story between her and her father, but he had picked up enough from her comments to guess the man had tried to crush the life out of her, for reasons he couldn't understand.

He didn't want her to go back to that. But how could he possibly ask her to stay here, where he had nothing to offer her but heat and bugs and his own lousy track record at relationships?

He sighed, turning his attention back to the ocean in front of their running lights. The night was cool and lovely. Off the starboard side, he could see a couple of dolphins keeping pace with their boat and he was almost tempted to wake Olivia to enjoy it.

After perhaps an hour, when he judged they were close to Matapalo and about to enter the Golfo Dulce, he suddenly heard another craft above the noise of Cesar's little fishing boat. He jerked around and saw a large vessel cutting rapidly through the water, coming from the direction they had just traveled.

Acting on instinct, Ren cut the motor and the lights, praying the other craft hadn't seen them. The cessation of sound must have awakened Olivia. Her eyes fluttered open and she pushed herself up to a seated position.

"What is it?" Her voice was rough, thready with sleep. "Why did we stop?"

"There's another boat coming fast behind us. I'm hoping they miss us in the dark."

"Do you think it's Rafferty?"

Her voice wobbled with fear, and he reached for her hand and squeezed her fingers. "Doubtful. There are a lot of boats along the peninsula. I just don't want to take any chances."

She still looked fearful, her fingers clutching convulsively in his. Poor thing. He couldn't help it—he pulled her into his arms and kissed her gently. "We'll be okay," he promised, though he hoped to hell he could keep that particular vow.

They sat together in silence as the boat approached them, perhaps thirty yards away on the seaward side now. It was lit up like a Christmas tree, every exterior light blazing. As it moved past them, his stomach sank. He could clearly read the words *Buena Suerte* on the side.

It was Rafferty's luxury yacht.

He held his breath, hoping against hope they were too far away for anyone on the other craft to see them. A moment later, a searchlight scanned the ocean and he suddenly heard a shout from the other boat.

"Mierda!" He pushed Olivia toward the other seat and fired up the motor again.

"It's Rafferty, isn't it?" she cried.

He nodded grimly.

"Can we outrun them?"

No chance in hell, he knew. Rafferty's yacht was sleek and fast.

"We can try," he assured Olivia. "Get down."

Out of shooting range, he meant, but he didn't say it as he fired Cesar's outboard as fast as it would go.

But after only a few moments, he knew it was pointless. The *Buena Suerte* wasn't going anywhere; it was now well within range. He kept waiting for bullets, but they never came.

Huddled on the deck of the boat near his feet, Olivia looked close to tears, white-faced and terrified.

They had come so close. How the hell did Rafferty keep coming out on top?

Since they weren't shooting, he wasn't about to cut

the motor anytime soon. Jimbo could damn well follow him straight to Golfito.

Someone on the deck of the *Buena* was yelling and waving his arms. A moment later, he heard an amplified voice coming from speakers on the yacht.

"Stop, Dr. Galvez. Stop now!"

It wasn't James Rafferty's voice. He didn't know who it was and he didn't much care, but at the sound, Olivia's head came up. She stared at him for a long second, then swiveled her head around to look up at the much larger craft.

"Stop immediately," the voice called again.

In the approaching dawn, he could see shock in her deep blue eyes.

"Stop, Ren! Stop!"

"No way!"

She clambered to her feet and stood with the wind whipping her hair behind her, staring up at the other boat. He hit a wave, rocking the boat, and she wobbled a little.

"Liv, sit down," he ordered. "You're going to fall out."

"No. You have to stop!"

She was so insistent, almost frantic with it. Though he fought the inevitable with every fiber of his being, he knew they couldn't keep up this pace. Sooner or later the yacht could cut in front of them, and he would be going too fast to avoid a collision.

With his heart pounding, he cut the motor and the little fishing boat slowed. Olivia continued to gaze up at it, that stunned disbelief in her eyes.

"F-Father?" she called. "Is that you?'"

A man leaned over the higher deck of the *Buena*. He

looked bluff, distinguished, with a shock of white hair and broad, commanding features.

"Olivia? Oh, thank God. Are you hurt?"

"I…no. Not really. Wh…what are you doing here?" Olivia asked.

"Chasing you halfway across the ocean, it feels like. Come aboard. You're safe now."

Ren didn't know exactly what was happening but something drastic had changed in the last few minutes. Her father was on James Rafferty's yacht? None of it made sense.

"Where's Rafferty?" he called. "This is his boat."

"I borrowed it from him to look for my daughter. I'm sure he won't be needing it for some time."

"He won't?"

"He's in the custody of the Costa Rican Rural Police, held on assorted charges of murder and attempted murder. Now, please. Come aboard."

"You had best listen to him."

This suggestion was uttered in Spanish. Ren looked closely as another man leaned over the railing.

"Manny?"

"*Sí.*"

A weight the size of Olivia's home state seemed to lift from his shoulders as he heard his old friend's voice. Relief washed through him. If Manny Solera was aboard the *Buena Suerte*, Olivia would be safe there. Manny wouldn't let anything happen to her.

With the oar, he maneuvered their smaller boat to the ladder on the port side.

He tied up alongside it and held a hand out to Olivia to help her climb.

He followed right behind her and by the time he reached the deck, he found her in an awkward embrace with the stern-looking man he assumed was Wallace Lambert.

"Father, what are you doing here?" she said after a long moment. "I don't understand."

"You should. You brought me here."

Color soaked her cheeks and she stepped away, looking forlorn. "I'm sorry. I made a mess of things, as usual, dragging you down here to bail me out of trouble."

From all she had told him of Wallace Lambert, Ren would never have thought the man capable of gazing at his daughter with such deep emotion, but it was unmistakable in his blue eyes, a much paler shade than his daughter.

Wallace reached into the pocket of his tan slacks and pulled out a cell phone. "Listen."

He pressed a button and a moment later, Ren heard James Rafferty's voice, distorted on the voice messaging system.

It should be easy. I'll just make it look as if when I caught you both and tried to transport you to my estate to await police, Dr. Galvez tried to escape, killing the both of you in the process. It will be tragic, really. You were so close to safety.

Ren stared at the cell phone, baffled. "Where did that come from?"

Olivia looked stunned as she pulled her cell phone out of the pocket of her dress.

"I hit Redial while you were still unconscious. I thought I was calling your friend, Detective Solera. I suppose that's you."

She turned to Manny, who nodded, his eyes slightly dazzled.

"Instead, she called me," Wallace Lambert said. "I was in the air but my voice mail picked up. I got the message the moment my plane landed in Puerto Jiménez. Some of the message was garbled, but I heard that part loud and clear and put the pieces together from the rest. I know James Rafferty planned to kill you both."

"I can't believe someone heard me! I thought the battery was dead!"

Manny stepped forward and spoke in his heavily accented English. "We knew from the phone message that Rafferty was taking you to Suerte del Mar. *Señor* Lambert insisted we immediately stage a rescue."

"He…he did?" She blinked, clearly stunned.

Wallace Lambert's mouth tightened and he looked even more stern, as if he hated his daughter knowing of his concern. Ren wanted to shake him.

"Sì. Sì," Manny said. "We took two helicopters to Suerte del Mar. When *Señor* Rafferty returned for this boat to look for you, we waited for him. After we arrested them, one of his men told us you escaped on a small fishing boat. It seemed fitting we use Rafferty's yacht to find you."

Olivia looked as if she could hardly believe what had happened. The sun was beginning to crest the inland hills and in the pearly morning light of dawn, she was radiant, fresh and lovely.

And absolutely not for him.

She turned to him and the joy in her features made his chest start to ache again.

"Nice work, Liv," he said, forcing a smile.

"There's coffee in the galley," Wallace Lambert said in the brusque voice Ren was beginning to realize was customary for him. "Come down and you can tell me what you were thinking to go off without telling me."

He led the way to the three or four steps leading below deck without waiting to see if she followed. Olivia gazed after him, then back at Ren.

"Go on," he urged. "I need to talk to Manny anyway and catch him up on our side of things."

She looked torn for just a moment, then she nodded and followed her father. As he watched her go, he wasn't sure what hurt more—his head or his heart.

Chapter 15

This all felt wrong.

She should be deliriously happy. She and Ren were both safe, James Rafferty would have to pay his karmic debt after all, she had a cup of delicious Costa Rican coffee steaming between her hands and she was on her way back to civilization.

And, stunning shock of all shocks, her father had been worried enough about her safety to come to Costa Rica looking for her.

She still couldn't quite fathom that one. She wasn't sure she would ever get over her stunned disbelief when she saw him on the deck of Rafferty's yacht, looking down on them with worry in his stern eyes.

She hadn't realized what a terrible burden her fear had become until it was lifted from her shoulders. And while she was almost dizzy with relief that no one would be shooting at her again anytime soon, she couldn't shake the conviction that things had changed drastically between her and Ren.

He had barely looked at her since they climbed aboard the *Buena Suerte*. He had been distant and cool, as if the arrival of her father and Manny Solera and the conclusion of their terrifying ordeal was not at all what he wanted.

She had no idea why he was acting like a polite stranger, but she had come a long way in the last few days and she wasn't about to let him shut her out. Not anymore.

They were nearing Puerto Jiménez when she finally broke away from her father's astonishing solicitude and headed to find Ren.

She found him on deck, leaning against the railing and gazing out to sea, still wearing the tan cargo shorts and navy golf shirt he'd borrowed from his friend's closet in the bungalow.

He looked darkly gorgeous, male and dangerous and very unlike any scientist she had ever imagined.

He gave a half turn when she walked up from below deck and watched her approach, an unreadable expression on his features. She leaned against the railing and watched the sea rush past the swiftly moving yacht.

The silence between them felt odd, constrained. They had never had trouble talking while they were running through the jungle, but now everything seemed different.

He was the first to break it. "Your father isn't quite the ogre I pictured."

"He's not, is he? He apologized to me for the whole Bradley thing. Can you believe that? I don't remember my father ever saying he was sorry for anything. He said he made a terrible mistake trusting him, and he was proud of me for doing the right thing and breaking the engagement."

"Good. That's just what he should have said."

"You know, it's strange. After all we went through, I feel like I'm seeing my entire life through a different kind of lens. As if everything I thought I knew about myself has been shaken around and put back together."

She lifted her face to the sea breeze. "I have spent so long feeling as if I would never measure up. My father has rigid expectations for himself and everyone around him. I was so busy feeling inadequate, I never realized he loved me despite my failings."

"You're not inadequate, Olivia. I hope you realize that."

He didn't call her *sweetheart* or *baby* or *Liv*. His formal use of her full name seemed just another stone in the wall he was building between them.

"I do realize that now. I'm only sorry it took a traumatic few days to show me." She paused. "I suppose you're eager to return to your turtles. Olive Ridleys, right?"

He seemed surprised she remembered. "Yeah. *Lepidochelys oliveacea.* I'm expecting an *arribada* sometime soon."

"That's when thousands of females come ashore at the same time to lay their eggs, right?"

He blinked. "Right. How did you know that?"

"It's amazing what you can learn on the Discovery Channel."

He smiled a little, though it wasn't anything like the broad, delighted grins he'd given her at random moments over the last few days. "*Arribada* means arrival in Spanish. It's an amazing thing to see. Thousands of females—sometimes hundreds of thousands—cluster offshore, waiting for more and more turtles to gather. We don't know why they finally decide the time is right, but they suddenly start to come ashore in waves—sometimes so many, there's no room for more nests and they start digging up others to lay their own. We think it's a survival mechanism. A saturation effect. When they reproduce in such mass numbers, it's impossible for predators to take all the eggs so it increases the odds that more will survive."

He glowed when he talked about his work and she envied his passion. "I hope your research hasn't been compromised because you've been away from it for a few days."

"I should be okay. I might need to tweak a few things here and there, extend the data collection dates, but I can figure it out."

His voice drifted off and again they lapsed into awkward silence. She hated this. With a physical ache, she mourned the loss of the closeness they'd shared back at the bungalow, those incredible moments in his arms. She had no idea how to gain them back.

"I guess you've had a pretty unforgettable honeymoon," he finally said.

"There are some things I can't wait to forget." She met his gaze intently. "Others, I will remember the rest of my life."

A muscle tightened along his jawline. After a moment, he jerked his gaze away and looked back out to sea. She would have given anything to know what he was thinking but he seemed as impenetrable as a sea stack.

He was pushing her away and there was nothing she

could do about it. She didn't know how she could scramble back. "Ren, I…"

Her voice broke and to her horror, her eyes filled with tears. He looked down at her for only about half a second, then he pulled her into his arms. He was solid and warm and wonderful and she wanted to stay here forever.

"Don't, Liv," he murmured. "Don't cry."

With effort, she choked down her tears, focusing on the hard beat of his heart beneath her cheek. This might be the last time he ever held her, and she didn't want to ruin the moment by blubbering all over him.

"I'm sorry," she finally murmured. "It sounds so trite, but I have no idea how to thank you. What does a woman say to the man who saved her life a dozen times? Everything seems completely inadequate."

"You know what you need to do. Just go back to Texas with your dad. Patch things up with him, chase your dreams. You can do anything you put your mind to, Liv. These last few days have proven that without question."

She laughed raggedly, wiping away a lingering tear. "You just might be the first person in my life who's ever believed that."

"Not anymore. Now there ought to be at least two of us. If anybody ever gives you cause to doubt it again, you just smile that Southern belle smile of yours and sweetly tell them you've faced off with a fer-de-lance, climbed a hundred-foot tree and ziplined through the jungle in pitch darkness. You can do anything you want to do and if they don't believe it, they can just go to hell. That ought to shut 'em up."

She managed a tremulous smile that slipped away

when he gave her a kiss on the forehead that seemed painfully like a benediction.

"Drop me a line when you open your restaurant."

He stepped away and though the morning sun was already warm, she shivered at the absence of his heat.

"Is this it, then?"

"That's Puerto Jiménez right there. We'll be docking in a minute. I imagine we'll have to give more formal statements to Manny, but you and your dad can be headed home in a couple of hours."

He spoke casually enough, but she was certain she saw shadows in his eyes. She opened her mouth to beg him not to do this, not to shut her out, but fear closed it again. She couldn't bear the idea of laying her heart bare for him and having him reject it.

She had endured a tremendous ordeal the last few days, but she was quite certain she wouldn't survive that.

It took most of the morning to give his statement to Manny at the police station in Jiménez. He knew Olivia was doing the same in another room.

Already, *La Guardia Civil Rural* had a powerful case against Rafferty. They had him cold on kidnapping charges and could probably make attempted murder charges stick if they could prove he'd fired on Olivia and Ren. Ren knew there was a chance he could try to wiggle out of those charges by saying his henchmen had acted too aggressively, but since two of those men had come forward willing to testify against him, it would be a tough sell.

Trying him on homicide charges for the woman Ren had watched him murder wouldn't be as easy, Manny told him, despite Ren's eyewitness testimony. They would probably never find her body—likely fed to the gators or dropped out to sea somewhere by now—which would make a conviction difficult.

But thanks to Ren and Olivia, they did have the identity of the man who had accompanied the woman to Suerte del Mar. If they could convince him to testify against Rafferty, justice might be within reach.

"That should be everything," Manny said. "But I have to tell you, the next time you decide to kidnap a tourist and drag her through the jungle, I'm afraid I cannot go as easy on you."

Ren mustered a smile as he stood. "There won't be a next time, I swear. I'll leave the tourist rescues to you from now on. I'm going back to my turtles."

"Smart decision. Though what you did was a good thing. It would have been a shame if Rafferty had harmed *Señorita* Lambert. She is a very lovely woman."

Inside and out, Ren thought, awash in longing to see her again.

He should go back to Playa Hermosa now, he knew. It would be safer that way, but he couldn't force himself to go without at least saying goodbye one more time, wishing her well on her journey home. It was the polite thing to do, he told himself.

"Where is she?" he asked with a deceptive casualness he was quite certain didn't fool his old friend for a moment.

Solera's eyes darkened with sympathy. "Probably on her way back to the States by now. I'm sorry. Her father was taking her straight from here to the airstrip. They left a few moments ago."

Ren let out a breath and gripped the back of his chair

tightly. He shouldn't be surprised. He had made it clear enough on deck of the *Buena Suerte* that there was no room in his life for her. He had urged her to go back to Texas and build a life for herself and he had no business now feeling so devastated that she'd taken his advice.

His head throbbed where Rafferty's goon had hit him, and his stomach felt hollowed by loss. He was miserable already and she'd only been gone a few minutes. How in the world was he going to live without her the rest of his life?

"Do you need a ride back to Playa Hermosa?" Manny asked.

He shrugged. "I'll catch the *colectivo* to Carate in a couple hours."

"We can probably find a cot for you here at the station to rest until then."

He shook his head. Right now, the only flat surface he was interested in was the polished bar at the cantina across the street.

Though it probably wasn't a good idea for someone who had suffered a head injury just a few hours before, he didn't care. By the time the *colectivo* left Puerto Jiménez later that afternoon, Ren planned to be completely, hopelessly, thoroughly loaded, to forget for now about being on the wagon.

Maybe then this ache in his heart would fade.

A half hour later, he sat at the open-air cantina in question—mostly vacant since it wasn't quite noon—with an Imperial and a plate full of uneaten *bocas* in front of him.

He had a depressingly clear view of the airstrip from here and he couldn't seem to rip his gaze away from it. He had watched two planes come in, but so far nothing had left.

He might still have time to catch her, if he hurried....

It was a crazy impulse, but he still stood up at the exact same moment a small silver jet suddenly thundered down the runway and lifted into the air.

Ren stood and watched it soar into the drizzling rain until it was out of sight, then he slumped to his seat again. The lager wasn't hard enough, he decided. He told the barkeep to bring him a whiskey instead.

The man poured him one of the Costa Rican distilled varieties and he was just starting to raise it to his mouth when he sensed someone standing near him.

"I'm no doctor but do you really think whiskey's a good idea after a possible concussion?"

The glass froze halfway to his mouth. He knew that low, sexy drawl. Still not quite believing his ears, he turned slowly.

Shock and joy exploded inside him, and he set down the whiskey so hard some sloshed over the side of the glass. "You left. I just watched your dad's plane take off."

He couldn't seem to stop looking at her. She'd changed out of the cotton sundress she'd borrowed from Bobbi. She was wearing another dress, this one lavender with tiny dark purple flowers and undoubtedly expensive.

"I decided I wasn't ready to leave yet," she murmured, and he forgot all about what she was wearing.

"No?" he managed.

"Nope. There are still things I want to do here."

"Such as?" His voice sounded as if he'd swallowed a handful of bitter genipa berries.

"I haven't been to Corcovado National Park, which I've heard is spectacular."

He let out a shaky breath. "What else?"

"Well, I haven't seen an *arribada* yet. I've been assured by the pre-eminent turtle biologist on the Osa Peninsula that it's a can't-miss event."

"True enough."

She paused and gave a small smile, though he thought he saw nerves in the rich blue of her eyes. "And I haven't yet spent an entire night in the arms of that turtle scientist, who, I should probably tell you, just happens to be the man I'm in love with."

Her voice trembled a little on the last few words, and she lifted her chin as if bracing for somebody to deck her.

Ren stared, stunned into speechlessness, even as a fierce joy burned through him. He wanted to reach for her, just sweep her into his arms and drag her back to Playa Hermosa, but he knew if he touched her, he wouldn't let her go.

"You can't be in love with me, Olivia," he finally said. "We've only known each other a few days."

She shrugged. "I've lived at least two or three lifetimes in those few days. I don't need more than that to know what kind of man you are."

He shook his head. "You don't have any idea what kind of man I am. I'm selfish and thoughtless, completely committed to my work. Sometimes I get so busy working I forget to eat. I'm a bear to live with, Liv. You need to go back to Texas. That's where you belong, where you're comfortable."

"I'm not. I don't belong there. I never have."

"You don't even like Costa Rica!"

"It's growing on me. I've been told it's a different place in the dry season. I'd like to find out."

"What about the restaurant you want to open?"

"I've got this crazy idea. Tell me what you think. Why can't I open a restaurant here on the peninsula? A nice little place on the coast that serves good, home-cooked meals to tourists and locals alike?"

He wavered for just an instant. The idea of having her here, building a life with her, planning a future, was heavenly. He had a vivid image of her bustling around a busy kitchen while he sat at a table telling her about some discovery he'd made that day.

He wanted that ideal to come true, with a fierce ache that stunned him.

"You'd be miserable in a week," he tried again. "You know you would. You're used to an entirely different life. You said it yourself. You're no nature girl. You can't stay."

She stared at him for a long moment. He thought his words were getting through. Then she planted her hands on her hips and spoke in an exaggerated sweet magnolia kind of voice.

"Excuse me, sir, but I won't let you tell me what I can or can't do. I've faced off against a fer-de-lance, I've climbed a hundred-foot tree and ziplined through the jungle in the pitch dark. I can do anything I want to do, Ren Galvez, and if you don't believe that, you can just go to hell."

He heard his own words from earlier that morning bounced back at him. As he stared at this small, curvy woman, with her indomitable strength and courage, something shook loose around his heart. The last layer of carapace shattered and drifted away.

He couldn't live without her.

It was as simple as that.

He loved her, and it seemed the height of stupidity to push her away when she obviously didn't want to go anywhere.

"I can't go to hell," he said. "I'm already there, or at least I was until you walked in. My plan was to get good and drunk and maybe I could drown this pain in my chest at the thought of you leaving."

"I don't want to go, Ren," she whispered.

He couldn't help himself. He pulled her into his arms. Her arms slid around his neck and she sighed his name when he kissed her. He closed his eyes, overwhelmed with tenderness.

"It ripped my insides out to say goodbye," he admitted softly.

She smiled against his mouth. "I love you. I know you think it's too soon, that I don't know you well enough, that I can't possibly be sure of my own mind. But I do love you, Ren. You saved me in a hundred different ways."

His arms tightened and he kissed her again.

"Those are all the reasons I told myself why I couldn't possibly be in love with you," he answered. "They make sense on an intellectual basis. A lasting kind of love takes time to develop. It can't come from a quicksilver few days when everything was wild and intense. My head knows that. But a good scientist also knows when to throw out intellect and go with his gut. This is one of those times. I fell head over heels for you that first night when you started climbing that tree, even though you were obviously terrified of heights."

She smiled, his soft, curvy little bombshell. "You promised you wouldn't make me do that again. I'm holding you to it."

He kissed the corner of that smile, more in love with her by the second. "I won't," he repeated his promise. "But can I still teach you how to kayak?"

She tilted her head, considering. "Can you give my arm muscles a few days to recover from climbing first?"

"You can have as long as you want, sweetheart. We've got all the time in the world."

She smiled with radiant joy and wrapped her arms tightly around his neck. As Ren picked her up with an exultant laugh and carried her out of the cantina into the tropical rain, he knew she was right where she belonged.

* * * * *

Welcome to cowboy country...

Turn the page for a sneak preview of
TEXAS BABY
by
Kathleen O'Brien
An exciting new title from Harlequin Superromance
for everyone
who loves stories about the West.

Harlequin Superromance—
Where life and love weave together in emotional and
unforgettable ways.

CHAPTER ONE

CHASE TRANSFERRED his gaze to the road and identified a foreign spot on the horizon. A car. Almost half a mile away, where the straight, tree-lined drive met the public road. He could tell it was coming too fast, but judging the speed of a vehicle moving straight toward you was tricky.

It wasn't until it was about two hundred yards away that he realized the driver must be drunk…or crazy. Or both.

The guy was going maybe sixty. On a private drive, out here in ranch country, where kids or horses or tractors or stupid chickens might come darting out any minute, that was criminal. Chase straightened from his comfortable slouch and waved his hands.

"Slow down, you fool," he called out. He took the porch steps quickly and began walking fast down the driveway.

The car veered oddly, from one lane to another, then up onto the slight rise of the thick green spring grass. It just barely missed the fence.

"Slow down, damn it!"

He couldn't see the driver, and he didn't recognize this automobile. It was small and old, and couldn't have cost much even when it was new. It was probably white, but now it needed either a wash or a new paint job or both.

"Damn it, what's wrong with you?"

At the last minute, he had to jump away, because the idiot behind the wheel clearly wasn't going to turn to avoid a collision. He couldn't believe it. The car kept coming, finally slowing a little, but it was too late.

Still going about thirty miles an hour, it slammed into the large, white-brick pillar that marked the front boundaries of the house. The pillar wasn't going to give an inch, so the car had to. The front end folded up like a paper fan.

It seemed to take forever for the car to settle, as if the trauma happened in slow motion, reverberating from the front to the back of the car in ripples of destruction. The front windshield suddenly seemed to ice over with lethal bits of glassy frost. Then the side windows exploded.

The front driver's door wrenched open, as if the car wanted to expel its contents. Metal buckled hideously. Small pieces, like hubcaps and mirrors, skipped and ricocheted insanely across the oyster-shell driveway.

Finally, everything was still. Into the silence, a plume of steam shot up like a geyser, smelling of rust and heat. Its snake-like hiss almost smothered the low, agonized moan of the driver.

Chase's anger had disappeared. He didn't feel anything but a dull sense of disbelief. Things like this didn't happen in real life. Not in his life. Maybe the sun had actually put him to sleep....

But he was already kneeling beside the car. The

driver was a woman. The frosty glass-ice of the wind-shield was dotted with small flecks of blood. She must have hit it with her head, because just below her hairline a red liquid was seeping out. He touched it. He tried to wipe it away before it reached her eyebrow, though, of course that made no sense at all. Her eyes were shut.

Was she conscious? Did he dare move her? Her dress was covered in glass, and the metal of the car was sticking out lethally in all the wrong places.

Then he remembered, with an intense relief, that every good medical man in the county was here, just behind the house, drinking his champagne. He found his phone and paged Trent.

The woman moaned again.

Alive, then. Thank God for that.

He saw Trent coming toward him, starting out at a lope, but quickly switching to a full run.

"Get Dr. Marchant," Chase called. "Don't bother with 911."

Trent didn't take long to assess the situation. A fraction of a second, and he began pulling out his cell phone and running toward the house.

The yelling seemed to have roused the woman. She opened her eyes. They were blue and clouded with pain and confusion.

"Chase," she said.

His breath stalled. His head pulled back. "What?"

Her only answer was another moan, and he wondered if he had imagined the word. He reached around her and put his arm behind her shoulders. She was tiny. Probably petite by nature, but surely way too thin. He could feel her shoulder blades pushing against her skin, as fragile as the wishbone in a turkey.

She seemed to have passed out, so he put his other arm under her knees and lifted her out. He tried to avoid the jagged metal, but her skirt caught on a piece and the tearing sound seemed to wake her again.

"No," she said. "Please."

"I'm just trying to help," he said. "It's going to be all right."

She seemed profoundly distressed. She wriggled in his arms, and she was so weak, like a broken bird. It made him feel too big and brutish. And intrusive. As if touching her this way, his bare hands against the warm skin behind her knees, were somehow a transgression.

He wished he could be more delicate. But he smelled gasoline, and he knew it wasn't safe to leave her here.

Finally he heard the sound of voices, as guests began to run around the side of the house, alerted by Trent. Dr. Marchant was at the front, racing toward them as if he were forty instead of seventy. Susannah was right behind him, her green dress floating around her trim legs.

"Please," the woman in his arms murmured again. She looked at him, the expression in her blue eyes lost and bewildered. He wondered if she might be on drugs. Hitting her head on the windshield might account for this unfocused, glazed look, but it couldn't explain the crazy driving.

"Please, put me down. Susannah… The wedding…"

Chase's arms tightened instinctively, and he froze in his tracks. She whimpered, and he realized he might be hurting her. "Say that again?"

"The wedding. I have to stop it."

* * * * *

Be sure to look for TEXAS BABY,
available September 11, 2007,
as well as other fantastic Superromance titles
available in September.

HARLEQUIN®
Super Romance®

Welcome to Cowboy Country…

TEXAS BABY

by Kathleen O'Brien

#1441

Chase Clayton doesn't know what to think.
A beautiful stranger has just crashed his
engagement party, demanding that he not
marry because she's pregnant with his baby.
But the kicker is—he's never seen her before.

Look for TEXAS BABY and other fantastic
Superromance titles on sale September 2007.

Available wherever books are sold.

HARLEQUIN®
Super Romance®

**Where life and love weave together
in emotional and unforgettable ways.**

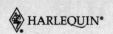
HARLEQUIN®

EVERLASTING LOVE™

Every great love has a story to tell™

Third time's a charm.

Texas summers. Charlie Morrison.
Jasmine Boudreaux has always connected
the two. Her relationship with Charlie
begins and ends in high school. Twenty
years later it begins again—and ends again.
Now fate has stepped in one more time—
will Jazzy and Charlie finally give in to
the love they've shared all this time?

Look for

Summer After Summer
by
Ann DeFee

**Available September
wherever books are sold.**

www.eHarlequin.com

REQUEST YOUR FREE BOOKS!

2 FREE NOVELS PLUS 2 FREE GIFTS!

Silhouette® Romantic

SUSPENSE

Sparked by Danger, Fueled by Passion!

YES! Please send me 2 FREE Silhouette® Romantic Suspense novels and my 2 FREE gifts. After receiving them, if I don't wish to receive any more books, I can return the shipping statement marked "cancel." If I don't cancel, I will receive 4 brand-new novels every month and be billed just $4.24 per book in the U.S., or $4.99 per book in Canada, plus 25¢ shipping and handling per book plus applicable taxes, if any*. That's a savings of at least 15% off the cover price! I understand that accepting the 2 free books and gifts places me under no obligation to buy anything. I can always return a shipment and cancel at any time. Even if I never buy another book from Silhouette, the two free books and gifts are mine to keep forever.

240 SDN EEX6   340 SDN EEYJ

Name	(PLEASE PRINT)	
Address		Apt. #
City	State/Prov.	Zip/Postal Code

Signature (if under 18, a parent or guardian must sign)

Mail to the **Silhouette Reader Service™**:
IN U.S.A.: P.O. Box 1867, Buffalo, NY 14240-1867
IN CANADA: P.O. Box 609, Fort Erie, Ontario L2A 5X3

Not valid to current Silhouette Intimate Moments subscribers.

Want to try two free books from another line?
Call 1-800-873-8635 or visit www.morefreebooks.com.

* Terms and prices subject to change without notice. NY residents add applicable sales tax. Canadian residents will be charged applicable provincial taxes and GST. This offer is limited to one order per household. All orders subject to approval. Credit or debit balances in a customer's account(s) may be offset by any other outstanding balance owed by or to the customer. Please allow 4 to 6 weeks for delivery.

Your Privacy: Silhouette is committed to protecting your privacy. Our Privacy Policy is available online at www.eHarlequin.com or upon request from the Reader Service. From time to time we make our lists of customers available to reputable firms who may have a product or service of interest to you. If you would prefer we not share your name and address, please check here. ☐

Silhouette®
Romantic
SUSPENSE

COMING NEXT MONTH